THE

EMBROIDERED

SHOES

THE
EMBROIDERED
SHOES

STORIES

CAN XUE

TRANSLATED BY
RONALD R. JANSSEN AND JIAN ZHANG

Henry Holt and Company
New York

Henry Holt and Company, Inc.
Publishers since 1866
115 West 18th Street
New York, New York 10011

Henry Holt is a registered trademark of
Henry Holt and Company, Inc.

Published in Canada by Fitzhenry & Whiteside Ltd.
195 Allstate Parkway, Markham, Ontario L3R 4T8

Library of Congress Cataloging-in-Publication Data
Ts'an-hsüeh, 1953–
[Short stories. English. Selections]
The embroidered shoes : stories / Can Xue ; translated by Ronald
R. Janssen and Jian Zhang.
p.   cm.
Translated from Chinese from various sources.
ISBN 0–8050–5413–8 (alk. paper)
1. Ts'an-hsüeh, 1953–   —Translations into English.   I. Title.
PL2912.A5174J34   1997
895.1'352—dc21   97–2227

Henry Holt books are available for special promotions and
premiums. For details contact: *Director, Special Markets*.
First Edition: 1997

Designed by Claire Naylon Vaccaro

Printed in the United States of America.
All first editions are printed on acid-free paper.
1   3   5   7   9   10   8   6   4   2

TO

QINGYIAN ZHANG

AND

TO

ALFRED JANSSEN

In Memoriam

CONTENTS

CONTENTS

ACKNOWLEDGMENTS

Several of these stories have been published previously in Chinese and/or English. The following stories have appeared in the mainland Chinese journals noted: "The Embroidered Shoes and the Vexation of Old Lady Yuan Si" in *Seagull* (海鸥, *Hǎiōu*), November 1986; "Apple Tree in the Corridor" in *Bell Mountain* (钟山, *Zhōngshān*), June 1987; "Two Unidentifiable Persons" in *The Writer* (作家, *Zuòjiā*), February 1989; "A Strange Kind of Brain Damage" in Special Economic Zone Literature (特区文学, *Tèqūwénxué*), January 1990; "The Child Who Raised Poisonous Snakes" in *Harvest* (收获, *Shōuhuò*), June 1991; "Anonymities" in *Beijing Literature* (北京文学, *Běijīng wénxué*), March 1994.

In addition, the following stories have appeared in the U.S. literary journal *Conjunctions*: "The Embroidered Shoes and the Vexation of Old Lady Yuan Si" and "The Child Who Raised Poisonous Snakes" in issue 18 (1992); "Two Unidentifiable Persons" in issue 21 (1993); "A Dreamland Never Described" and "Anonymities" in issue 23 (1994); and "Homecoming" in issue 28 (1997); and an excerpt from "Apple Tree in the Corridor" has appeared in *Grand Street* (1997).

THE

EMBROIDERED

SHOES

THE
EMBROIDERED SHOES
AND THE VEXATION
OF OLD LADY YUAN SI

My neighbor, old lady Yuan Si, is a garbage collector. Though her business is nothing more than picking up trash, she is an iron-willed old dame.

Not long ago, old lady Yuan Si started to terrorize me. Every night after I turned off the light, this woman would barge in, her hair disheveled. She'd ransack my bedroom, smashing mirrors and cups, and then the light reflecting from the shards would drive her into a rage. She'd tear my quilt from the bed rudely and stare into my eyes with a flashlight for a long time. After all this, she would pee right there in the middle of my room. I was totally exhausted by her incursions, which were causing me to grow thinner and thinner, and weaker and weaker, day by day, until finally I was nothing but skin and bones.

Once I tried to lock my door and even pushed a table up against it to block it. As a result, she could only scream and shout outside. Then she found a hole and started to dig away at the brick wall of my house making heart-stopping, thunderous sounds. In the end, I had to open the door and let her in. Another time, I locked my door as early as dusk and hid myself in my neighbor's house and slept the whole night. Early in the morning I returned home. As soon as I opened the door she dashed in ahead of me. It turned out that she had waited throughout the night just outside my house.

Suddenly she stopped coming, and this lasted for more than ten days.

Tonight she came on schedule, but she behaved differently. She hopped about on one foot for a while. She giggled and laughed in the darkness, then suddenly took off her shoes and sat on my bed. She grabbed my shoulder with one hand and with the other she chopped at me with force. It hurt so much that I jumped up in pain. Then she said, "The most difficult part is persistence, hey?"

". . ."

"The whole truth about this business is going to be revealed, and I am overjoyed! Have you noticed the shoes I'm wearing?"

"Huh?"

"Let me tell you about it in detail. For more than ten days, I've been hunting for them in your room. I was suspicious of everyone and felt terribly upset. It was not until recently that an idea came to me out of the blue: I would adopt a strategy of subtle indirection—and unexpectedly the problem has been completely solved. The focus of the problem is this pair of shoes, this pair of shiny, brilliant embroidered shoes. This pair of shoes is the fate of my life. Now that the objects have returned to their original owner, everything will be as clear as daylight. Justice will win a victory and the bright sun will shine over my head . . ."

"So you mean you don't need to come to my place anymore?" I asked hesitantly, secretly hoping for a positive answer.

"Why not? How can you be so naive? So insensitive? From now on I will come every day and tell you the story in detail. There's a host of little details. Whenever I think of getting the chance to tell others about it from beginning to end, I become so excited that I tremble. This is like a secret in a treasure gourd that cannot be told in half a year or even a whole year. Now I've found something interesting to do!"

She shouted with joy and sat down right on my chest. Taking out that damned flashlight, she studied my eyeballs. I became dizzy and muddleheaded and felt a yellow coating develop on my tongue.

"I'm a garbage collector," she said slowly, taking her flashlight away. Her glance was vague but emotional. "When she was young, Old Lady Li was also a garbage collector. Later on she became successful. Do you know why? This involves a profound question. And the question is rooted in this pair of embroidered shoes. Please look carefully at this pair of shoes."

Using one foot she dug underneath the bed for her shoes. She tried for a long time, and then she showed them to me with her flashlight. They were no more than a pair of rotten wooden thongs.

"What do you think of them? Aren't they a pair of magic shoes? I have a kind of premonition, a kind of confidence.

Now I need only close my eyes and all of those things that happened in the past seem as though they took place just yesterday. As I lie here concentrating, the tears begin to flow.

"The thing happened on an April day. Even now I can smell the fragrance of the earth. Early in the morning, I was about to leave the house dragging a willow basket behind me. Then she came. Her face was rosy—she was a TB patient and her face was never red, but that day, I don't know why, her face was really rosy. She stared at me meaningfully for a while and suddenly raised the issue of borrowing my pair of embroidered shoes. At the time, you know, I was young and naive without any idea of the viciousness of the sophisticated world. Of course, I lent the shoes to her without hesitation. I was even hoping she would ask me for something else. The rooster was crowing outside the door, and I was so touched by my own generosity that my eyes became all red. I wanted to jump up and embrace her.

"At that moment, a gentleman passed by my window. He was a buyer for the salvage station. He glanced at *me* attentively with a kind of moist look that resembled a drizzle. I'd bet he was even in a daze for a while. Why should he look at me? Why should he look at me instead of her? Why should his glance go through her to look at me? I did not understand at all at that time. I was too pure, as pure as a pool of water.

"That night I slept soundly. In the morning when I woke up I heard the hooting of an owl and I found myself in a bad mood. It turned out that everything had changed unexpectedly in my dream. It turned out that evil had defeated virtue and the devil had won the crown. From that day on, our female swindler rose to success!

"From that day on I fell into an abyss thousands of feet deep. Out of my wits, I ran to the door of her straw hut and drummed on it with all my might. I drummed and drummed until the backs of my hands were swollen. Suddenly I raised my head and found that the door was locked. There was a small slip of paper tacked on the door that read HOUSE FOR RENT. I fell to the threshold and cried out.

"Out of nowhere that day there came a swarm of wild cats. No matter where I went they followed me, meowing incessantly. I was heartbroken and cried endlessly. Some passersby stopped, feeling sorry to see such great sorrow in such an innocent little girl. And our swindler had become a respectable character! Who could see through such a vicious fraud? Much less would they know there existed such a pitiful little victim. The embroidered shoes that she had made with hardship and sweat had become the tool by which vicious people might deceive others.

"You have to understand that the buyer for the salvage station has remained in the dark even up to this day. Several times when he saw me he was stunned and then went into a trance as if lost deep in a vague and distant memory. This meant that at that time he had totally confused the two of us, and he mistook the woman swindler for me. He had fallen into a love that was not returned. He was simply too honest. Like me he never understood the sophistication of the world and human beings. He knew only generosity. She had enchanted him completely. And the main factor was, of course, my embroidered shoes. Once she put on that pair of shoes, she became unrecognizable.

"My heart was shattered. For several days, I was so low that I could neither eat nor sleep. Intentionally, I made myself ugly. In my rags I would clutch my willow basket and wait outside the door of the buyer. As soon as they appeared, I would scream at the woman, 'Deception will eventually be seen through!' That vicious whore pretended not to recognize me at all. With one arm she held that mummy and ran off like a dog. That buyer had been turned into a mummy. She had destroyed him completely. I was so pained and regretful that I beat my chest and stamped my feet in the rain. Stretching my neck, I howled like a female wolf.

"Other times I chased them down the street, throwing banana peels and broken bottles at them. Every time the buyer would flee, towed along by that whore. He sobbed and his head drooped like a dead bird's. Sometimes while chasing them I slipped and fell in the mud. The rags and papers in my basket spilled out over my body. I struggled up and continued my chase until I caught them. Then I stopped them and glared at the whore, asking pointedly: 'How are your shoes?'

"Time flew by, one year after another. Wrinkles spread across my face one after another. I was told that the swindler had been promoted to accountant. When I heard the news I felt so disheartened that I passed out. While collecting garbage in the wilderness I would bump into that buyer once in a while, that old man with senile dementia. Every time he would look startled as if he were about to awaken. I wondered if there was some kind of conditioned reflex in that brain of his, which resembled a mess of porridge. Maybe he felt a puff of warm steam? Maybe he thought he saw a light shining through the dim passages in his idiotic brain? The brief glance in front of the window . . . Oh, oh! He had lost his mind completely, pitiful guy!

"The year I turned fifty I was determined to take revenge. I wanted to make this historical scandal public. I wanted to find my shoes and use them as solid evidence, to administer a humiliation that the whore could never wash off.

"At the beginning I used the strategy of direct attack. Repeatedly I dashed into their house to search around in the dark of night. But that whore was very cautious. Every time I came back empty-handed. In addition there was that damned mad dog. That dog never barked but jumped out and bit people from unexpected dark corners. Even today, there's a scar on my calf. That was part of the evil trickery of that swindler. She pretended to be sound asleep and she never dared to turn on the light for fear of showing her shameless face. At those moments I did not ransack the place when I dashed in. Instead I made an especially disturbing sound hoping I would give her a nervous breakdown.

"For several years I continued with this strategy. Then one rainy night, the thunder rolled so loudly that one question leaped into my mind: Could it be possible that she had transferred the shoes to someone else's house? Could there be a secret partner here? I started my attack and search in different households, never letting one night go by—I have long cultivated the habit of not sleeping at night. There was no sign of progress in my work and I couldn't see any hope. Heavy dark clouds enveloped me. During those melancholy days I wavered, and I even thought of committing suicide. I became so pessimistic and world-weary that I would hide myself indoors, crying and stamping my feet. I even broke windows without any reason and shot passersby with my air gun.

"In the final critical moment I adopted the strategy of indirection as my single venture. I stopped going out and collecting garbage and I stopped my hunting at night. When I met others I declared that I was suffering from some serious illness and I put on an air of being in pain. I even sent a little child to the drugstore to buy medicine. Day after day I observed the outside world attentively through a crack in the curtain. Blood throbbed in my veins, and my heart pounded madly in my chest. Oh, day after day, day after day, I encouraged myself continuously: 'What should happen is going to happen, it's going to happen!'

"When the blue glow brightened outside the window, when I was moved to tears by the heroic struggle in my life, the truth all of a sudden was exposed in the light of the day! This is truly a miracle of mother nature, an unthinkable miracle!

"Tonight I feel a little bit tired and I'm going to sleep at your place. Wait until tomorrow evening—I'm going to tell you the shocking details. I'm going to tell you in great detail."

And then she started to snore loudly.

TWO

UNIDENTIFIABLE

PERSONS

It was Lao Jiu (Old Vulture) who led him to see that man. Passing through a dense willow forest, they found him amidst a pile of dried-up weeds on the riverbank. His face covered with a ragged straw hat, he lay on his back sound asleep, the toes on his bare feet spread wide. Lao Jiu pulled him down and thus the three lay together. Soon afterward, they saw the waterfall plunging overhead.

"There's a landslide quite near here," Lao Jiu harrumphed. "That guy, he understands everything. All doubt will come to an end here."

He started to make up a self-deceiving story. Recently such stories came to him automatically and turned in his mind like a revolving lamp.

The sound of bubbles breaking is a delicate one. You can only hear it by touching your ear to the earth. Is the sound of silkworms pulling silk for cocoons more delicate than that?

They had finally reached this place. For a long time, he'd had the feeling that Lao Jiu would lead him to see this man, but he had not guessed that the day would come so quickly. Now the thing had happened before he'd had time to pull the snarled threads of his confused mind out straight.

The day before, he had argued repeatedly with Ru Shu until they reached a kind of compromise. Clinging together, they stood in the chill wind probing for the image in each other's mind.

"Don't go," she said, laughing softly, a little to his surprise. "Of course, I'm going to write that kind of letter. You're going to receive a lot of them, piles of them, heaps. There's virtually no possibility for retreat."

Instantly, she vanished without sound or shape, as if she were a gust of cold, black wind.

He could not connect the feeling that she gave others now with the bright, sunny days of May. Before the coming of those days every year, he would be sleeping soundly. The naughty children in the neighborhood would take that chance to break his window in broad daylight. When the broken glass hit the floor, he would tighten the quilt around his body, pretending to be a silkworm swinging his head. He was the sort of person who is mentally a little bit slow. He did not count the disappearance of Ru Shu as starting at that time. Instead, he insisted stubbornly on reckoning it from a day five years later. The very concept of time was distorted in his mind. This was unexpected even to Lao Jiu.

Lao Jiu had also produced letters, though never in written

form and never received by him in the mail. However, in those long five years, he had reread those letters constantly, and he knew that Lao Jiu had never let him go.

On the riverbank all sorts of feelings welled up in his heart, and his body felt extremely fragile as though with one slight movement he would fall into pieces. His brain was delicate and juicy, like a tiny melon sprout. Lao Jiu always disdained his brain, never considering it seriously. However, on this day stories streamed out of his brain like a flooding river. His hair hung down into the water. Each strand swirled in its own fantastic pattern.

"I'm not that disheartened," he started to think, with some reason. "Without parents and brothers it appears like that kind of thing. The matter is becoming clearer as time goes by."

"It's okay not to go," Ru Shu had said. Childishly, she stretched out a finger and drew a big circle in the air. "The blossoms of the broad bean are twinkling."

Before making the decision, the two of them had pried open the lock of a deserted house and lived there together for three months. The house stood at the very end of a deep, empty lane whose dim and narrow path was piled with rotten leaves. At the entrance of the lane, there shone a tiny electric light that never went off all year round. Every time he entered the lane, he had to fend off a sudden attack of horror. The door was always ajar. Ru Shu insisted that once the door was closed the air pressure inside the room would become so great that her temples would swell with pain. She acted like a deranged person—she feared light, sound, air currents. All she did every day was huddle in the dead air.

"This is such an evil place," she would say, lying in his bosom, trembling. She felt as hot as a lump of burning charcoal. "It's our bad fortune that we have stumbled into such a place."

With much pain and difficulty they held out until dawn. He suggested that they change to another place. All of a sudden, Ru Shu's white teeth started to shine. Raising her eyebrows fiercely, she declared that she would continue to stay in this house—this good place. If he could not stand the atmosphere, he didn't have to come anymore. After all, he was not predestined to live in such a ghostly place. But she was different. She considered this house as her foreordained abode. Everything in the house was simply wonderful! The pitch of her voice reached higher and higher, and became a string of shrill notes scattering in the air. In the dim rays of the morning sun, he saw a swaying mottled shadow. From that moment, he made the decision in his mind. This house was not an easy place to make a decision.

The process of splitting up was very painful. Ru Shu stayed in the corner all the time. She refused to step out of the door even during the day. He was determined to consider her behavior as arrogant and presumptuous. Secretly he plotted an insidious and vicious revenge. During those days of stalemate, Ru Shu asked him if it was possible to exist in this world as a ghost of oneself. Take her, for instance—now that she had realized her destiny, would it still be possible for people (including him) to live with her? In the past when they had lived with her, could it be that she was never with them in reality? After she and he had escaped from the mass of people, her life had become simple and under her own control. Could everything that had happened in the past be nothing but illusory models?

Stroking her shoulders, he spoke aimlessly some irrelevant words of comfort. Meanwhile he pondered his scheme for revenge. He believed with indifference that the final solution was approaching. His stroking fingers gradually folded into an iron-hard claw as she sank into desperation. Moving into this house could be her last struggle. This reminded him of a verse for a famous ancient poem: "Amidst dark willows and bright flowers, there appears another village."

Ru Shu had not been too happy at the beginning. Standing at the doorway for a long time, she had hesitated to enter the house. Listening attentively with her head tilted to one side, she rattled on and on that it would be too early to live here. Maybe it would still be okay without moving in. Would this be too reckless? Would it be more reasonable for them to hide separately in some populous place? Once they had entered the house, both of them would be exposed to each other's scrutiny. There could be some hidden perils. He knew that she was always prescient. Yet he lost his head so completely in his own zeal that he did not realize the implications of her remarks.

Quickly Ru Shu became active. Once the light was turned off, her rich imagination poured forth a stream of increasingly complex images. She would talk and talk, putting on all kinds of expressions and gestures, as if she were in a performance. As all her unique linguistic features were transformed, every word became transparent and elusive. He knew that, yet he did not want to consider this to be his only life. Since childhood, he had placed higher expectations on himself. Therefore, he left the house early every morning and returned late at night. Upon his departure every day, he could feel Ru Shu's eyes glued on his back. Gradually she lost all sense of his existence and instead indulged herself in daydreaming. When he returned, she would spin around and smile at him reluctantly, pretending to be calm and indifferent. "Your face is covered with spiderwebs." She would start the conversation with this same remark every day. Then she would cut off her talk right there.

One night, he made it appear that he was asking her casually what she had done during the day. She chuckled and said she had been extremely busy. During the day she had jumped down from the trains at least six times, and this had caused a crack on the sole of her foot. This could be considered a sign of aging. In the early years this used to be such an easy thing. "By the way, I took time to look at our tree," she said seriously. With pain, he listened to her lies. Surprisingly, he found a side in her temperament that previously was completely unknown to him. It was obvious that she had never left the room. Staying in the stale air had caused purple spots on her face, and her fingers were getting bonier each day. Only her hair remained as thick as before. It could even be considered full of vigor. Those nights when he had his attacks of fever, he loved to press his cheek against this tender and icy cool thing.

During the day he spent most of his time sitting dully with Lao Jiu in a pavilion in the middle of the boulevard. Although Lao Jiu knew his situation perfectly well, he kept silent. Lao Jiu knew exactly what the matter was with him. He would fool around until dusk before going back to that house. He was so afraid that Ru Shu would see through his tricks during the day that he would scrub the soles of his shoes loudly on the palm bark doormat, pretending that he was weary and worn from a long journey.

"So you're back!" Ru Shu would jump up like a cat, and put her arms around his waist from the back. "I'm simply worn out. I ran a greater distance than a horse could cover today. Are you listening?"

She appeared tiny, fragile, hopelessly dependent, and pitiful. Thinking of Lao Jiu's facial expression, he couldn't help shaking his head.

Nobody knows the history of Ru Shu. It seems that she has been living on this piece of land since ancient times. This has left traces of a faint ironic smile in her eyes. Her random, irrelevant talk always makes people uneasy. As a matter of fact, people have neglected her over the long years. When she reached the age that she could understand her place in the world, she started to exploit her ambiguous position and single-mindedly go her own way. It was exactly from that moment that people started to stare at her body with surprise. Nobody knew where she was from nor how she had come to be like this. Much less did people know what kind of person she would become in the future. It was also at that moment that he met her on the street. Probably that was the prime time for Ru Shu because she was swollen with arrogance, charged with aggression, and full of self-indulgence. Or it might be called naivete and childishness, or perhaps treachery and disgracefulness, or still other things.

During his lonely adolescence he had all kinds of expectations for himself. He believed that during his life he would associate his fate with a certain woman of the same type. He considered himself as belonging to a unique "kind." Therefore, when he found Ru Shu he was rapturous. Probably their relationship was established only because neither of them had any doubts about it. They met on an old bench in a park. At the moment he was dozing off in the glow of the setting sun. Then all of a sudden here she came. She was both thin and light, resembling a willow leaf. She seemed as if she were waiting for someone impatiently. She would stand up and look around repeatedly. After a while he realized that the woman did not really sit on the bench, but in the air about an inch and a half above its surface. He blinked his eyes with force several times to confirm this unique fact.

"Those things that everybody considers as counter to reason happen to me every day."

When she was talking she did not turn around. Instead she sat quietly in the air. There was nobody else around. Obviously she was talking to him. Only gradually did he begin to focus on her words. He felt goose bumps on his body, and a string of strange associations poured into his mind one after another. The woman kept her back to him, making all his efforts to determine her appearance in vain. It was not until much later that he remembered again to examine her. And then he found that she had appeared in his memory frequently for a long time.

"Ru—Shu," with effort he pronounced her name. "Where are you from?"

His breathing became heavier, and his pupils dilated. In the thickening dusk her silhouette appeared floating and unstable. An old man made a crackling sound sweeping the fallen leaves. It seemed that something inside him exploded, and all at once his face turned white as a sheet. "Wait a minute!" She was running so fast that she might have been flying. Afterward he joked to her that he had never chased a woman like that before, nor even a man. He wondered what kind of feet she could possibly have. Sitting on his lap, she answered, deep in thought: "I have very similar feelings, but I really do have weight. You can feel it, can't you? This is a never-ending test."

Occasionally she would sink into deep thought. (In fact, it was not deep thought but only empty-mindedness. But to others she appeared to be deep in thought.) At those moments her eyebrows became extremely long. In addition, she wiggled her ears like a little kitten. Finally under the pear tree in front of that house, she told him what kind of woman she was and he also told her what kind of man he was. They were longing to give each other a feeling of reality. The descriptions were incoherent, but clouds of dazzling color floated in them. Almost simultaneously they said the sentence: "You are the person who has been living with me all the time. Together we observed the nests of the birds in the forest." The leaves above them rustled in the noon sunlight, bringing them a feeling of peace and security.

He couldn't make clear his own history either. He did not consider this question until he was thirty. And the more he thought about it the more confused he became. Yet through this confusion there appeared a feeling of purity and newness. When he talked to Ru Shu about this, both of them felt extremely relieved.

"Once in a while I enjoy making something up," Ru Shu said. "Nobody needs to make things up. We may suppose that the incident happened on a long, empty street, between the two lamps. This sounds very dramatic. According to others, everything has a beginning. You and I cannot come to this world from nowhere. My job is to knock on strangers' doors at midnight. I often ask myself: 'Why should I do this? How do I know there are people inside? Is this a genetic inheritance?'"

"As a matter of fact, starting from the very beginning we two are in a somewhat dubious position," he said. "They have told me the limits on me, which seem to have something to do with being a scholar or something like that. Occasionally, I think about the rules, but the next minute I'm capricious again. I have even forgotten how Lao Jiu came into my life. It probably had something to do with my history. Starting from now on, you can observe him, Lao Jiu, attentively. This is a vital matter. You see, I can forget about him so easily. I am forever so careless and undisciplined. In my impression Lao Jiu has been there from the very beginning, like the legs on my body."

Casually they wandered on the pebbled road that burned in the sun. Deep inside they hoped to find some trace of something related to present matters that could provide a new passion to the stories they made up. But they also knew that its arrival would be for the most part accidental. It was not at all necessary for them to pursue it purposefully. They only needed to wait. Beside the road sign there was a dark shadow. It was none other than Lao Jiu. A man and a woman passed by them quickly. The man was rattling on: "The truth of the matter disappears like a stone sinking into the vast sea. Everything relevant to it remains in silence. To sum up, the whole thing is a swindle. Here we have too many similar things. It's time to call an end to it. Why should we look into the straw hat that a certain man threw away on a rainy day in a sudden impulse? Only when we observe this world in silence can we gain real enthusiasm."

A train was passing by. Its whistle made Ru Shu jump up, startled. Standing for a long time at the original place, she waited until the last car disappeared in the distance.

"I jumped down from that train. There was an eagle painted on the gate of the car. At the time you said to me, 'It's marvelous.'" She continued as if enchanted, "That can't be wrong. It's been stored in my newest fresh memory. There might be a day when I would take a walk with you as we are now. We would be very close to each other. Lifting my feet I would jump up. I was good at chasing the train, and I should have told you about it long ago. How is it that there's always a railroad at the place where we take a walk?"

She praised him lavishly for his being able to struggle out her name from absolute emptiness.

"Very few people have the ability to do that. This is an outstanding work of youth. Everyone is involved in the cheap trick of getting to the bottom of things, while you have almost reached the height of a flying horse galloping in the sky by your own sheer animal strength."

He was determined to exclude Lao Jiu from the world that belonged to Ru Shu and him. His mind was made up from the very beginning though he had no expectation about the effect. Lao Jiu was one to worry about. He always maintained a great distance between them, keeping his mouth shut but knowing everything. In his mind Lao Jiu belonged to existence in the prehistoric period—barren, solemn, and indestructible. He needed him as much as he needed Ru Shu, except he never needed to express it outright. Whenever he thought of Lao Jiu, he would appear, every minute, every second. By contrast, Ru Shu never appeared at his expectation. Every memory of her came in incoherent flashes. She explained that this was because she had constantly been in chaotic transformation.

"It might get better when I grow older." Her tone was mournful.

Lao Jiu did not do anything. Every day he did nothing but wander around. He never knew how he had managed to make a living till now. Ever since he could remember, he had seen Lao Jiu wandering around. He appeared to be an ageless man with ice-cold glances. He had no emotional relationship with anybody in this whole world. Once, brazen faced and unreasonable, he had persisted in following him to his house. It was an empty house. The windows were surrounded by withered evergreens. As soon as they opened the door, an old man in rags sneaked in. He looked so much like Lao Jiu that he could have been his father, although Lao Jiu denied it firmly. He screamed at the old man, "Scram!" There was no bed in the house nor quilt nor anything like that. Where did he sleep at night?

Lao Jiu saw through his doubt. Winking, he laughed in his direction. "Only a fool goes to sleep. But I am an extremely wise fellow."

When he sought a reason for it, he had become a friend of Lao Jiu's because they had some cruel essence in common.

He had an uncle who was a very headstrong man. When he walked he raised his head high and took giant strides. At night he never turned on the light. Stubbornly, he would sit in the middle of a dark room. Every time he wanted to turn on a light, his uncle would *humph* coldly, making him retrieve his hand in mid-reach unconsciously. Afterward he felt so angry that he cursed his uncle again and again whenever he remembered him. Yet this still wouldn't lessen the hatred. Once a brainstorm hit him, and he tricked Lao Jiu into going to his uncle's house. He didn't even try to turn on the light. From the beginning his instinct told him that such behavior would not fit Lao Jiu's manner, and he admired it greatly. Without expressing any emotion Lao Jiu moved a chair in the darkness and sat himself down side by side with the mountainous uncle. He hid himself outside the window and watched this dumb show.

One hour passed. Two hours passed. Finally the uncle jumped up in a rage. Turning on the light he yelled at him hidden behind the window: "Where did you pick up this bit of a clown? You heartless wolf! Hey?" He was so furious he didn't know where to focus. His eyes were bulging.

When he told Ru Shu about this, the two of them laughed so hard that they almost lost their breath. Ru Shu called the uncle a "burly chap" and Jiu a "pangolin." When these two words slipped from her mouth smoothly, he felt completely relaxed and he couldn't control his joy. Ru Shu had her particular names for every person and every thing sur-rounding her. She usually spoke them in a casual way, and then both of them were full of a kind of evil excitement. She had never seen the uncle, yet she could create accurately from her mind the uncle's pet phrases, such as "Small potatoes have small potatoes' ideals; they don't feel the least bit less than others" or "Nobodies are all involved enthusiastically in a competition of personalities. This world is creating genius," et cetera. Her re-creations made him totally wide-eyed and dumbfounded, believing sincerely that the devil had entered her body. The third day that he got to know Ru Shu she told him that she could not exist with his friends in one world. Lao

Jiu had an evil look—there would come a day when he would kill her.

"But Lao Jiu is not everywhere, we can easily abandon him."

"But in reality he is you, how can you abandon yourself completely? Forgetting is only temporary, swayed by personal feelings. In a moment he would come back again. The person that is going to accompany you all your life will be him and not me. Yet we have to try, because you are my only one."

So they started their experiment. They ran far away. They built a tent in the middle of the desert and roasted lamb. Both of them made themselves dusty and muddy, and both of them were burned black by the sun. They appeared healthy, natural, and unrestrained.

One midnight Ru Shu woke him by pushing hard. He heard her screaming: "He's here!"

"Who?"

"Who else can it be?!" Her face was white as a sheet.

Sitting at the desk, she dripped red ink one drop at a time onto the stationery. Those were secret codes that could never be interpreted. Afterward she went to the well to wash vegetables. A train ran by, and she jumped onto it. In the five days since she disappeared, he and Lao Jiu could barely leave each other. In his sorrow and emptiness, Lao Jiu could always give him a certain kind of real feeling. The two of them sat in dull silence. They wandered and they dozed, thinking of something gloomy and ambiguous. Finally, they stared at each other and smiled in understanding.

Soon Ru Shu came back. She said that she had made only a short trip because she was feeling bored. Now everything had returned to normal. He shouldn't blame her for it, should he? Such temporary separations could not be avoided between them. Now everything was returning to normal and she begged him to please believe her. She dragged him to the pear tree. The rustling of the leaves warmed his blood. Because of the thrill of reunion, both of them had that kind of alien yet familiar feeling. Ru Shu said she would not abandon Lao Jiu anymore, and now she understood it. When the train took her afar, she felt closer to him.

He said in a flattering tone, "I have run through a lot of train stations looking for one with a painted eagle. Even in my dreams the train wheels were rumbling."

Lao Jiu did not change the least bit because of Ru Shu's reappearance. In his memory nobody else's image had forced itself into his mind besides this fragile companion. He could not see her. Obviously he could not see anybody. During the days when his companion was warmly involved with Ru Shu, he sat amidst the maple trees on the mountain observing his chest, which grew older every day. He even stamped a little green poisonous snake to death with his bare feet. Bathing himself in the sun, he could feel that the poisonous juice inside his body was filling up day by day. He thought of how odd and unique the means of communication were that he had with his companion. This was mostly accomplished by aspiration. Thus his companion could get him whenever he called him.

Contrary to the other two, Lao Jiu had no doubt whatsoever about his own birth history. He had never revealed to anybody his own belief. He only tried to blend a unique manner into every deed. When his companion mentioned with excitement his own ambiguous position, considering it an honor, he only glanced at him sharply, fluttering his eyelashes.

The old man finally had a general explosion. Locking the door, he started wrestling with Lao Jiu. He said, puffing hard, "Some gratitude for decades of raising up the child. . . . Such a plot in broad daylight!"

With ease Lao Jiu threw him out the window. Then patting the dust from his clothes, he thought of the endless greed of human beings—and the inexplicability of their desires.

His birth was the product of a plot that happened in a quiet ancient residence. He accepted the matter in the year when he was two. Among a group of naughty children, he discovered his companion. The gloomy glance of that child attracted him immediately. Without the child knowing it, he entered his life and became another soul of his. The endless path toward his destiny was empty. It had been his dream to have a young and confused companion. In secret he would guide him to the termination of his journey. He would be the only person that he could remember in the world. Before his appearance, his mind had been vacant for many years. Inside, there were only a few monkeys swinging on dead branches.

"We fall into sleep under the shining stars, and we wake up in the morning glow; in our visions lions run in the jungle."

In drifting terms he described to the child the scenery at the termination.

"But this place is falling into dilapidation day by day. Within one year you won't be able to distinguish seasons, and within one day you can't distinguish day from night. The sky is forever a bleak grayish white. There's neither jungle nor people. Gradually even you will be turned into a red-color-blind patient. Just look at that floating leaf. What kind of exaggerated gesture!"

The teenager was forever bent over his black leather notebook, his face full of scars of memory, the gloomy expression in his eyes hiding a desire to murder. Lao Jiu was waiting, and the chance was getting closer day by day. On the day when he reached his adulthood, he incited him to throw the notebook that his father had given him (Lao Jiu could still remember the youth's father) into the garbage can, thus fulfilling the wish that he had had for several years. From that day on the youth was severed from his memory and became an unidentifiable man.

Obviously this left artificial marks on his body. He was not born this way, but he didn't know at all that it was all Lao Jiu's arrangement. He only kept feeling surprised.

"I should have a father. This is very strange."

"The notebook that you have forgotten is his biggest mistake. The old man has cut off his own retreat."

The marks and scars on his face healed gradually, and the

shape eventually stabilized and many unpredictable expressions appeared. Sometimes his glance would startle Lao Jiu at a particular moment. Several times, he raised the issue of the black leather notebook to probe him. The teenager listened without any facial expression. Obviously he was changing day by day.

More and more often, he could hear his upset footsteps in the wilderness at midnight. The footsteps bothered Lao Jiu, making him get up, put a shirt over his shoulders, and listen. From the window he could see a swinging candlelight. The young man was alone. In the small hut behind him there were all kinds of groaning sounds. Originally, he had hoped for a companion, who obviously was not Lao Jiu—had hoped for not the present existence but some discovery. He felt he would die if he couldn't discover something new. Every day he despised his present existence. He would die of anxiety if some unexpected happiness did not appear. For several months he sat on the benches in the park half dreaming. He was trying to create a kind of strong image, yet simultaneously his mind resembled a dying rabbit. Ru Shu entered his life at that critical moment.

Ru Shu was a woman without roots. He noticed this while sitting on the bench in the park, and it was further proved when she repeatedly jumped from running trains to meet him. But this was not important. The thing that deeply shook his belief was the fact that she had her own pursuit.

"The cold wind blew and blew at midnight. I knocked open a door. From inside stretched an unfamiliar head. All of a sudden it started to talk. I could barely understand it at first, and I made all kinds of mistakes. Now that naivete has passed."

This was her description of her work. She said that up to now she had seen the goods in every house. There was no way to cheat her even if they wanted to. For example, the uncle. She had certainly seen him. Even with her eyes closed she could imagine him; otherwise, how could she give such an accurate judgment? Talking about him, she had also knocked at his door on a certain summer night in a certain year. At that time both of them were young, a little girl and a little boy. They were farther from resembling each other then than now. She remembered the incident. The reason she went to the park was because of her remembrance of this. At first glance she could see the changes that had taken place in his face over these years and the horror came to her. Then there was the incident of escaping.

"Why should you knock at the door? Since there is no secret whatsoever inside the house?" he asked.

She answered that it was because she did not want to give in, or she didn't want to lose the game. Since she had already entered the dead end, she had to bother the people inside the house for the rest of her life. That was all her happiness.

That fall, Ru Shu's searching gradually showed a purity and extremity. In the aging season, her face showed some edges and corners, and her expressions turned indifferent and cold. She came to him less and less; instead she would stay inside the house alone—her house was never located permanently at one place, and he could never decide where she lived. Like their life histories, it was a fabrication.

Using a charcoal pen she drew many thick lines on the wall (those walls were very white and totally empty), and on every line she drew numerous antennas. She told him that those antennas were all memories about nights. Now she was devoting all her energy to this work. Nothing related to daylight could arouse her interest. Of course, daylight did not include him. He also was an antenna that she had drawn, and he belonged to the night. This was revealed by the shadows in his face. Even the blazing sun in the vast desert could not burn that shadow away. The symbols on the walls were all alive. Very often she was so touched by them that she could not stop sobbing!

In a ceilingless house, she pointed at the slim woman who passed by outside the window and said, "She's wearing such a thin coat. Yet in the place she is going to it is snowing. The whole sky is full of six-cornered floating flowers. She is walking gently, taking into her eyes all the scenery along the way. 'Fragrant Grassland,' the name of the place, appears in her mind. But in reality the place in front of her is seeing falling temperatures. When I was young, I had similar experiences several times. Every time I forgot to bring proper clothes. Now that woman is far away, and her figure from behind does not appear that confident."

"Fragrant Grassland! Fragrant grassland in a snowstorm?" she suddenly shouted.

At the same time he found himself in the middle of a

crowded square. Many familiar faces passed by without expressions.

Somewhere Ru Shu was saying excitedly, "I'm the puzzle inside the puzzle!"

He knew what emphasis she made with her vigorous charcoal pen. He could also see her lonely destiny. He did not pity her, but let her go her own way. The narrative about that woman had started before they moved into the room in the corridor. For a long time, Ru Shu would toss and turn in bed, placing her fevered head on his bosom, and then she would lead into that story. According to her that woman was everywhere. She wrapped her head in a kerchief with colorful patterns. She would appear from a dark doorway and she would travel through every big street and small lane. She had been to Ru Shu's room. Quietly she sat by the desk and one page after another she turned through an old book, her ears pricked up with caution.

"Every time I removed the clutter from the desk, there was always one book that appeared punctually. In the light, her hair was shining, and it was even thicker than mine."

She asked him to recall from which day the story about that woman started. And he answered that it seemed to have started from that day when the camellia blossom withered away. That day they were circling around and around in the mountains carving their names in the bamboo. They didn't return to their house until very late. She was so sad that she couldn't go to sleep the whole night through. Sitting up she told him the story touchingly. She said that the woman had disappeared thirty years ago. Sitting by the window she finished reading one letter, then she walked out and disappeared amidst a vast sea of men. Left over on the windowsill were two glasses, one blue, one white, with tea marks inside.

"Thirty years is not that long," Ru Shu tried hard to explain patiently. "That woman would come every day because she belonged to a kind of eternity. Time had long ago stopped for her. Is it kind of dull to talk about this?"

She became very nervous and stared at the doorway. She was waiting for the knock on the door.

A
STRANGE KIND OF
BRAIN DAMAGE

There does indeed exist a strange kind of brain damage.

I have a friend who is a housewife in her thirties. When she talks with others, her left eye will not stop blinking.

One morning several years ago, this friend stopped at my door to tell me, "I'm suffering from some kind of illness. Unfortunately, nobody has noticed this. May I call this illness a form of brain damage? In my opinion, this is a special kind of affliction."

She leaned close to me and began fervently to describe her symptoms. More exactly, she was describing her daily routine. To be honest, I heard nothing unusual or even interesting in her discourse. She was the virtuous wife of a husband who had an impressive income, and she had two sons. Her family had attained a middle-class standard of living. These were things I had already known for a long time. I was puzzled by the effort she put into detailing that which was commonly known.

"Maybe you feel that life is empty?" I tried to sound her

out. At that moment, she was in the middle of her chatter about some trivia, such as shopping in the vegetable market, stopping on her way to have a pair of shoes repaired, and bargaining with the shoe repairer.

"Please don't interrupt me!" Her eyes flashed at me angrily, and her speech rushed on like running water. At long last, after she finally brought her story to the end of her prolonged day when she crawled under her quilt to enter dreamland, she turned her head toward me and remembered my question.

"Please blink both eyes, old friend, if you think you understand my words. Perhaps you want to render some judgment about it, but you would be seriously mistaken! What did I say? Who can respond to the deeper meaning of what I say? I have a disease, not epilepsy but rather a kind of brain damage. My symptoms are invisible. Only through my tone can you sense them. This is why I have wanted to tell you all these things. I want to ask you if you understand."

Of course I did not understand. In fact, I did not think she had any particular tone. Her narration, again, did not exceed the ordinary. If I had to name some characteristics, I could only say that her talk was a bit overelaborated and too insipid.

"In fact I feel very nervous," she said. "Who can explain my illness? Nobody would believe my story. But one day I did experience an attack of the illness. The cause was a scarf belonging to the woman next door. It was a very cold day, and early in the morning it started to snow. When I noticed the figure of my female neighbor, I ran to my window to watch. As I expected, she was wearing that damned green scarf again.

"I had had an argument with her the day before, criticizing her for wearing that irritating thing. She fought back ferociously, and even suspected that I was jealous. Anyway, she felt that I was not behaving normally. I felt very regretful after the argument. Closing my door, I screamed and even smashed a thermos bottle.

"I had happened to see her from the window that morning, so I ran out and jumped on her, trying clumsily to pull her scarf away. She let loose a torrent of curses, even using insulting terms like 'whore.' She was much stronger than I. With one swing of her arm, she threw me to the ground. Then she left me there in a rage. From that moment, I diagnosed myself as a victim of brain damage. Of course the event of the scarf itself was not important. It only triggered the attack. I've had the illness all the time.

"Just now I've described to you one day in my life. Haven't you sensed any implications? Not at all? Oh, no, don't think that I'm unhappy with my lifestyle. On the contrary, I'm very satisfied. I'm only a little disappointed that nobody can sense the subtle implications in my tone. People interpret my words according to their own standards.

"I've had only the one attack—the fight with the woman next door. Of course, nobody saw it, and that fool would never be able to figure out what was going on. She thought I was jealous of her, meaning that I wanted to have an affair with her husband or something like that. I haven't had an attack for a long time."

Suddenly she appeared bored. She yawned in my face and then left hastily.

It was probably the third day after my friend told me about her illness that I suddenly remembered the story as I was passing by her house and decided to visit her.

She was sitting at the desk writing something. When I entered, she only raised her head briefly and greeted me coldly. Then she continued her writing, her pen moving with lightning speed. I glanced at the notebook and discovered that she was not writing words, but some mysterious symbols. After ten minutes or so, she put down her pen and uttered a long sigh of relief.

"You think that I'm boasting?" She studied me carefully, and her glance made me very uncomfortable. "Contrary to everyone's expectation, my being ill is true. I'm a practical person with extremely logical reasoning in life. You're the one who deliberately mystifies the situation." Her tone sounded pedestrian and dull.

"Why do you say so?"

"For example, you mentioned something about life being empty that day. You tried to locate the source of my illness somewhere in the external. You distorted things to justify yourself. You even pretended to be a psychologist. Isn't that an urban, petit bourgeois frame of mind? When you came in just now, I was wondering whether I had wanted to have an affair with the husband of that stupid woman. Nobody could prove it either way. If I didn't want the affair, what did I want? The only thing certain is that I smashed my own thermos bottle. I've never even met that fellow, the husband. But that's unimportant; the important thing is that I saw the green scarf, which led to my crazy behavior. I'm the only person in this whole world who went nuts over that scarf. Okay, so it's done, and I don't want to mention it again.

"Haven't you seen that I am sinking into a narrow trap? You still haven't? My illness is something like congenital heart disease, but it's not fatal. I feel it frequently. I've described to you my daily routine. Of course you didn't understand me. Who does? I'm too tired of the confusion, so I'd better stop right now. Let me tell you something in the form of a story: There's a certain person in a good family and living a comfortable life. However, she has one slight defect—a rare illness which is going to develop day by day. Yet it will never be fatal. Don't misunderstand me, and definitely don't make any inferences, because everything is contrary to common sense. That's the end of the story. You'll be surprised when I tell you that I'm willing to deteriorate from the illness. I would be horrified if one day I felt any sign of recovery. Every day I wait anxiously for that feeling of the onset of the severe illness. I've told you that I'm feeling tense. Thank God, I'm not waiting in vain."

After she finished her talk, my friend chuckled. Pointing at the closed door behind her, she whispered to me, "Recently an old fellow has been living with us. He's a ridiculous guy, full of ambition to chase after petty advantages. I can't explain problems like that. Right now I'm planning how to chase him away. Can you help me with some ideas?"

I frowned. Immediately she pulled her face straight and said, "Please stop being sanctimonious! I've told you I'm a practical person, I might even be very vulgar, or maybe snobbish. Don't ever have any illusions about me!"

The door suddenly swung open, and a panic-stricken old man appeared in the doorway. Of course, he was the woman's father. He stared at us for a long time while licking his palms comically. My friend made a mad dash toward him, shoved him into the inner room with a curse, "Goddam it!" and slammed the door. Then she opened her outstretched hands and declared with desperation, "You see, I'm having another attack."

By chance, I met this father on my way home from work. The old man told me that she was not really as snobbish as she said. She had been treating him very well and showed a daughterly respect, except that she was hot tempered. "But recently, a great change had occurred. She's started telling everybody that she is ill. Is this merely some excuse?" The old man looked around nervously and added quickly, "I don't think she is ill at all! Only those who let rats run free are mentally troubled. But she is raising two huge black cats with care. This shows how good our household is. Can you tell me why she would want to kick me out? Can you tell me?"

The old man shrank his bony body into a lump. Dandruff lay all around the collar of his worn-out jacket. He appeared very embarrassed and also deeply terrified by the unpredictable future. He was a petty clerk retired from some organization. His only daughter had received a good-quality family education. Now that his wife had passed away, and he had planned to pass his old age peacefully with his daughter and her family, this awkward situation had suddenly arisen.

He was no fool, and he would fight to protect his own interests. He would not allow his own daughter to take such liberties and run wild. How could a person do as she pleased just by declaring that she had some kind of purely fictitious illness? He had lived for seventy years and had seen many seriously ill patients. But they all had to obey the law just like everyone else, and they never shrugged off their responsibilities and obligations. They went to see doctors as scheduled, took the medicines the doctors prescribed, and never made a fuss. He had never seen an illness such as his daughter's, which didn't need doctor or medicine. So he felt disgusted whenever his daughter mentioned her illness, but she mentioned it every day, purposefully. The old man complained to me for a long time in the cold wind, until both of us were overcome by perplexity and alarm. We kept silent about what we had in our own minds and then bid good-bye to each other.

The ending came half a year later. In a small, lonely hut next to the highway, the old man died in his bed. People did not discover the body until three days later. Since nobody could determine the cause of death, it was recorded as a natural death due to old age. Only the son-in-law and the two grandsons took part in the old man's funeral service.

That night, my friend came to my house without invitation. She looked very tired and discouraged. She had lost all her former vitality. Shading the lamplight from her face with a palm, she smiled wickedly and spoke in a low voice:

"So that man has become the first victim. You've seen it. Who will be next? At midnight when the patrol passes the street, you can stick your head out of your fifth-story window and see. A soul-stirring murder is being brewed next to the fountain near the front gate of the park. A human figure will jump over the locked iron gate. The edge of a knife will shine like a flash of lightning, and he will drop to the ground with hardly a sound. The hunter will have been waiting at the pre-determined place. He will raise his knife without even check-ing beforehand. When he slashes down, his hand doesn't feel anything. He pauses only for slashing, and the pause is per-functory. A wail similar to that of a dying pig will last for only half a second. A meteor will fall in the cold, pitch-dark night. The frozen surface of the water in the fountain will be broken by the heavy corpse. The illness I suffer from is homicidal ma-nia."

She felt frightened and asked me time and again if I had locked the door. She even ran to the door to check herself. She hid herself in my house for three days, shivering all over, until her husband came to take her away by force.

After that, nothing much changed in her. I often met her in the streets on her way to the vegetable market. Holding her basket, she appeared calm. But in her pupils, I could see a lin-gering trace of hesitation. She became silent. When I talked, she would listen quietly with apparent attention. Yet I knew that she did not hear anything.

One day, when I was about to leave her after saying hello, she grabbed me and uttered clearly, one word at a time, "He has been admitted to the hospital."

"Who?"

"Who else? He! My husband! He's finished! I used the same knife as before. You'll know it if you go and look. The blood from the burst vessels in his brain will kill him. Who'll be next?"

So I went to the hospital. Her husband was in a coma. The patient in the next bed told me that X rays showed his stomach to be full of extremely fine steel needles, about an inch in length. The strange thing was that there was no bleeding. The doctors planned to perform a major operation on him that afternoon.

However, this husband recovered miraculously. The next day he left the hospital, and I saw him sitting at home as if nothing had happened. "They made a mistake," he apologized to me with a smile. "It was nothing but a flu."

When I met her again, the first thing she mentioned was my poking my nose into her business by going to the hospital. Then she said that since I was so nosy, our friendship had to stop. She didn't like for others to interfere in her private business. As a patient, she had the right to do something strange. She was sneering as she spoke, her facial expression very determined.

Year after year, we keep bumping into each other. But she never casts even a sidelong glance, as if I no longer exist. When I observe her in secret, I find her facial expression as calm as before, and her steps are very smooth. Indeed, in such a noisy city as ours, she doesn't appear conspicuous at all.

FLOATING LOTUS

One ought not close one's eyes to the awkward way the tender filament of a body stretches from its thin shell to pull itself across the crushed stones and rubble. By some distant predetermination the tomato-colored sunlight has been rendered inconsequential to it. The forest is dense and humid. Carnivorous mosquitoes breed batch after batch at the bottom of the well. Although heaven and earth equal it in their nakedness, they do not have its delicate shell. After crawling, it rests awhile, letting its soft body huddle inside, gathering itself for yet another furtive effort.

"Floating lotus, floating lotus . . ." These words sound clearly and pleasantly, making people forget the forest as sharp as knives and the pain as keen as if the blades were cutting through their skin.

"Can that which happens on Wednesday recur in a Sunday's nap?"

When time crawls like this, rough scales encrust its antennae. It's not that it prefers monotony, but that it is the servant of the transparent fluid recirculating through its body.

In fact, it, too, was born in the tomato-colored sunlight. The memory of that time has been so obscured as to make it impossible for any trace to remain. But one day when a bird chirped, it was startled for a long moment. It could see the mosquitoes doing their usual mad dance along the rim of the well, those old fancy dances that it had grown weary of watching.

A man and a woman debate above it. He claims it can be destroyed simply by spitting on it. She doesn't believe him. Both of them glare at it.

Now it is in an antique hut, where two middle-aged men sit back to back. Whenever one of them speaks, the resonance in his chest reverberates in the chest of the other, making his lips move involuntarily. In general, each seems to speak independently, yet each hopes that the other will talk as much as possible so that he himself can go on endlessly also.

A: Shouldn't it be thought a marvel to change kapok into a golden necklace? This is a metaphor for wealth often used in the past.

B: I've been feeling afraid of losing something. It could be my urban petit bourgeois consciousness that drives me to constant pursuit. Even though I'm not in good health, I am an essentially solid sort of person.

A: It's not right to have a goal. Only when you advance counter to it can you possibly return home in one morning.

B: Suppose we try being silent. I think you can feel the resonance all the same. I've already heard your resonance.

One man begins to fidget. At this instant, we can hear a variety of drumming sounds echo in the chests of both. The second man starts to thrash about until both of them are exhausted, hot sweat streaming down their heads. Then they both stop simultaneously and sit down back to back again on a bench.

Time flies. A whole season has passed. Yellow leaves drop onto the windowsill, three altogether, arranged neatly.

"There's no real reason for us to pose this way against each other, like that pet with the antennae. It is driven by a constant desire to find a piece of smooth, muddy ground covered with liver moss. Or at least other people see this as its desire. But in reality, what is the essential motive? What on earth is essential? Why should things be one way rather than another? The existent is manifold. For instance, against the reddish-orange sunlight the forest rises sharp as a blade. We are forever in pursuit of something, but in reality this is futile.

In the rubble outside the hut an old rooster pecks at it attentively. The rooster appears extremely anxious. It pecks while also digging with its claw, rolling the little lump back and forth and refusing to give up. From an outsider's point of view, this is a soul-stirring spectacle. One can sense that the little thing is not nervous. It simply shrinks stubbornly into its thin, tough shell in a gesture of resignation to its fate. This goes on for half an hour. Then the rooster lifts its head and crows toward the heavens and forgets about the little lump beneath its body.

There was a period when deranged winds swept back and forth from every direction and the dried-up land opened in cracks. Many people pondered this. They thought and thought.

Raising their proud heads, their saddened and indignant expressions could be perceived.

At the same time, it dreamed in its shell about more peaceful days. Even when it wanted to move a little, it never stretched its antennae too far. It couldn't see the green mossy land before it. The bright sun had no bearing on it. The forest had nothing to do with it either. The only pertinent thing was the place one or two feet away.

A mob dashed toward the forest of strange trees. The rooster crowed again, its feathers standing up on its neck, one foot stepping into the edge of the forest.

The two middle-aged men are still talking calmly, each one speaking independently. Whenever one of them stops, the other appears restless and finds more words to say in order to guarantee that his opposite will be able to respond appropriately. And this response spurs him to go on talking.

Before we know it, a second session is half gone. This one has passed more slowly than the first, and there are no yellow leaves to symbolize it. It might even be said that this second season is almost motionless.

Both men feel they have lost the urge for everything except talking about dull subjects in order to stimulate the other to continue the dialogue. Neither, for instance, can remember how long ago they had a meal. Even their curiosity has shrunk to the single concern with what word will be spoken by the other. To make the other speak, each must talk without stop. Such drill becomes a monotony. Besides, the sounds from their throats are not at all pleasant.

It seems there was a period of ambiguity when the edges

of things were not distinct. The human heart waxed fresh and vigorous as if just emerging from a morning bath. Distant birds began to hop about continuously, and the waves rolled in systematically.

Standing before the window, A said something inadvertent. Its long resonance formed its usual parabola in front of him.

At that moment the rooster was a tiny, light brown, fluffy ball. No clues to future developments could yet be discerned. All existence went along happily under the will of heaven. With the accelerating motion of nonexistence, unstable embarrassing details gradually displaced themselves.

A's words stopped performing their parabola and became a spray of hurried dots emitting a perfunctory tone.

It was just at that moment that the sun turned tomato red. Loaches squeaked with suffocation in the ditches. By beginning their experience simultaneously, the two men greatly reduced the terror they would have felt in beginning alone, and they settled into a state of calm.

Outside, at an indeterminate point, it crawls forward methodically. One can see its trace amidst the rubble. It has no goal because it knows not where it is.

Everything that at first seems trivial or ambiguous shows great significance later. Because this phenomenon is so vulgar, so monotonous, once one glances backward at its origin one cannot help falling into illusion—it seems there shines a certain spiritual light along the trail from which it comes. Illusion is no more than illusion, and no one can clarify a situation from its origin.

The two middle-aged men from nowhere have never shown the slightest emotion. With their trivial, ordinary hopes, they have been sitting back to back in this little room in the hut for many years. The disturbance of falling leaves cannot arouse their surprise. Their talk has no particularly new content, only cliches, simple and repetitious.

B moves his body, feeling again that it is too troublesome for A to walk to the window and speak there. In fact, it is totally unnecessary. In the past B hated using such expressions as "time flies by" in his talk. Whenever someone used such expressions, he would harrumph with contempt. Recently he has tried several times to talk in a non-speech mode. This method has often proved effective. Every time he tried it, A would produce a resonance to the object expressed with such a method, and these resonances were particularly good. In such moments, A would encourage secretly, "Please speak more and more . . ." And B would fulfill his mission in solemn silence.

It knows nothing about the two men in the hut. It has never had an experience like theirs. It huddles inside its shell, sinking into a soft, sound slumber. Each time it wakes up it crawls for a while. The scenery before it may be startling, but it crawls along calmly from stone to stone, then rests for a few minutes before stretching its body once more outside its shell. All this happens silently. Its body is too soft to make any noise. Because of the shell, it does not feel much, even when such as the rooster pecks at it ferociously.

Somebody wants to perform an experiment: to portray the image of its crawling on the same canvas with the two men in the hut. After the experiment the canvas is hung at the edge of the forest. Yet the reality of the matter does not change much at all. The three of them still follow their own courses independently. No trace of passing time can be detected in their development.

The experimenter does not give up. Standing on a pine branch, he shouts back toward the place below, dragging his sounds out very, very long. But if you stand inside the hut you can feel that the shouting outside has been blocked somewhere. They can't hear it, and it can't hear it. So the experimenter becomes grieved. But this remains irrelevant to them.

Then the experimenter thinks that at least the two men in the hut have some comfort from each other, whereas it is too pitiful. It was born silently, and it will die silently.

Yet the experimenter is wrong from the very start. It can never experience the fastidiousness of human beings. Dreaming deeply in its own shell is its highest enjoyment. When it is attacked, it has the ability not merely to elude disaster but to transform it into pleasure, as in the case with the rooster.

"That which happened last Thursday is bound to be repeated in the nap on Sunday, floating lotus, floating lotus . . ." the experimenter says with feeling. He turns his hesitant glance toward the tomato-red rays of sunshine.

No one knows when the canvas disappeared. The scene of the hut and the rubble becomes clearer, the loaches leap in the ditches.

We always assume things in accordance with our own will. For example, standing before the canvas we cannot help singing some lyrics. Then the earth sinks, the fire dragon dances fervently, our meditating gaze gradually turns profound. But one thing we are very clear about—past the rubble there stands a very ordinary hut. We can say that nothing can hide inside.

"Floating lotus," the experimenter intones again with deep feeling.

A

DULL STORY

Now that we're talking about it, I used to be a very good athlete, a marathoner. I even won some local competitions. You know I have good legs. But although I'm good at running, I do have a problem—I have no appetite. I eat very little every day. In the past two years, I've lost almost all interest in food. This is fatal to an athlete. Yet medical examinations find nothing wrong with me. The odd thing is that I can still run as energetically as before despite the fact that I'm eating nothing. I even won the women's championship in the provincial competition. It was on the day of that victory that I became sick. I immediately ran to the ditch at the back of the house and disgorged violently. Everything poured out of my stomach with the force of an avalanche. When I returned to the house after I finished vomiting, everybody commented on how terrible I looked.

From that day on, I stopped eating once and for all, because whatever I swallowed down, I soon vomited up again.

Everything was turned upside down in my eyes. However, this did not interfere with my training and running. I continued my physical exercise, though I became thinner day by day. I lost more than twenty-five pounds in one month, and I looked all the more strange. The members of my team all said they were afraid to see me running. They could hear the grinding of my bones as I ran. And my skin became transparent, so they could see the movement of the bones inside my body. This was too much, too horrifying to them. They hated to see me running, because they did not want to be scared. After much cogitation, my coach decided to send me home for re- cuperation.

So I returned home and lived with my husband and chil- dren. My life was easy but sluggish. Then one October day, my father-in-law came. He wore an orange plastic raincoat, and he was shivering with cold. After some blushing and modest declining of hospitality, he finally sat down on the sofa. But he firmly refused our offer of a dry towel and hot tea. With his aged, veined hand he wiped the rainwater from his head and face. Pointing at me with one finger, he said to my husband that the disease I was suffering from was a very unusual one. He found in the medical books that this disease usually occurred among females. It was caused by the distance between their inner vanity and the goal they were after. At the root of my case was the fact that my legs were unique. He could tell at one glance that I would fall miserably. It was un- fortunate to have such legs, and there were endless troubles awaiting me. He did not look at me even once while talking, nor did he allow my husband to put in one word. He simply rattled on and on. Like a wizard, he delivered all kinds of prophecies with his eyes crossed. Upon his departure, for some unknown reason, he made a strange sign to me with his hands, stiff with gnarled joints. It looked like both a gesture of ingratiation and a sign of threat.

"Hey, take it easy," he said.

Father-in-law came increasingly frequently. It started with visits twice a week, then every day. Every time he would bring with him a huge medical book on neuropathology. He had folded down the corners of many pages, so he could always find just the place he was looking for. Then he would put on his spectacles unhurriedly, and read aloud those sentences and paragraphs from the book. After his reading, he would wink at me lasciviously and say, "Vanity cannot bring any benefit in the long run." He firmly rejected our every invitation of staying for a meal as if he had been insulted.

Once I mentioned to my husband his father's strange behavior. He smiled and raised his eyebrows, saying, "Can't you see that he is desperate because of his fear of death?" When I pondered my husband's remark, I felt as if I understood something, yet I did not understand anything. One thing was sure—my father-in-law took an extreme interest in me, or maybe we could call it extreme jealousy and hatred. But why? We had had no contact with him. My husband had left home at an early age and never took his father very seriously. In fact, he seldom even mentioned him. What had disturbed the old man so much that he decided to come to our house to make such confessions? Was it because of my not-very-great fame in the athletic world? But why should my fame irritate him so much? This whole business was very puzzling.

After about three weeks, he came one day with some pills of different shapes made of Chinese herbal medicine. He suggested that I take all of them. Staring at me, he declared that such pills could "snatch a patient from the jaws of death." Of course I refused to take them. Then we fell into a real mess of an argument. Quite to my surprise, he slapped my face. In the flurry, I kicked him with all my marathon strength. He squatted down slowly, holding his belly, his whole body trembling. After a long time, he struggled up and limped home.

After three days, my father-in-law was admitted to the hospital. According to my husband, excessive melancholy had destroyed the old man's physical balance. He believed that the argument had been fatal to him. "He hit you only because he was afraid of death!" my husband said, looking pensive. "The fear of death can make one lose his reason."

We went to see my father-in-law, who was lying in bed unconscious. Once he came to, he would stare at us in a threatening way with his bloodshot eyes.

On the way home from the hospital, I suddenly felt something wrong with my legs—my left leg, it so happened. I couldn't bend it, as if something were growing on the joint. My husband carried me onto the bus. By the time we arrived home, I could no longer stand up. We've been to hospitals numerous times and have taken numerous X rays. But there appears to be nothing wrong with the bones. No doctor can explain the case. I figure the reason that nothing can be diagnosed is that I am extremely antagonistic to the doctors.

Could it be that I had some subconscious guilty feeling about father-in-law's illness? Did I feel regretful about my rude behavior at the moment of our fight? Not at all. When I kicked him, I felt the joy of mischief in my subconscious. When I heard he was sick, I was indifferent. I only felt that he looked funny lying in the hospital.

Another strange thing was that my appetite completely recovered after my legs became sick. I ate and ate every day. Soon a ruddy complexion returned to my cheeks. Every piece of news about father-in-law's critical condition gave me a feeling of relief. Although I could not return to the athletic field, I felt my life had become more meaningful, with my renewed appetite as the sign. Once in a while, I would remember the wizardish glances of my father-in-law and his talk about my legs. Then I felt a little bit uneasy.

One day my husband came home and told me, "Father is wrestling with the god of death for the last time." Then he said that if he told his father about the problem with my legs, the news would no doubt bring him back to life. But he did not intend to tell the old man. He did not tell me the reason. After a long silence, he said quietly to himself, "The struggle in the dark depths is spectacular. In no sense can an ordinary person reach such a place."

One year later, I became confined to a wheelchair. Ever since that happened, my visual and audial abilities have been developing rapidly. It seems that the world surrounding me has become a crystal palace, transparent and shining from morning to night. However, at the extreme depth of my vision there is a small, moving black spot similar to a colon in a piece of writing. One night when I woke up I heard a weak noise resembling the clawing of a rat scratching among scraps of paper. I did not turn on the light—because darkness has no existence for me. Looking straight ahead, I could see that the black dot had turned into a small torch that disappeared after bobbing up and down several times. That rat's noise grew steadily louder, until it became deafening. My husband was startled awake. Sitting up, he mumbled, "Father's dead, died just now. I didn't tell him about your illness." I could feel the hesitation in his subconscious, though it was only a flash. In the end, he had come around to my point of view.

My complete victory increased a certain feeling of safety in me. It seems that my father-in-law was too fragile to withstand a single blow. After he passed away, I became more and more contented with my life in the wheelchair. One day a doctor came and gave me a thorough examination. His diagnosis was that my legs were perfectly normal. Immediately he ordered me to stand up.

"But why?" I stared at him with hatred.

At this moment my husband came in. With great effort he explained to the doctor, emphasizing repeatedly the advantages of my life in the wheelchair, as well as the disadvantages of standing up and walking, and so on. Finally, he said, "It seems to me that it's good enough for her to be able to live like this. It is much more natural than her running the marathon in the past."

Blinking his eyes, the doctor was completely confused. After a while he stuttered, "Then why should you ask me to come in the first place?"

My husband said, a little annoyed, "I asked you to treat her cold. These days she has a slight cold. We would like you to prescribe some medicine. But as soon as you arrived, you started to treat her legs indiscriminately. You are too subjective."

The doctor wrote a prescription and left in a rage. After the doctor was gone, my husband said to me, "Take it easy. Now that father is gone, nobody will come and bother you anymore."

Once in a while I hear news of sports from the outside world, such as who has won the championship or placed second and so on. Such things have become like smoke and clouds from another world to me in the wheelchair. My mind is becoming duller and duller and stiffer and stiffer daily. Every day I wander around from this room to that room by pushing the two wheels with my hands. Sometimes, I even go out the door and circle around the houses nearby.

The years of my life in this crystal clear world have caused my body to become radiant. At the beginning it was a little bit phosphorescent, starting from the nails on my toes. Because of the shoes I had on, nobody could see it and it was nothing. Finally, the day came when my husband told me that my legs had disappeared completely from his sight. From a distance I looked like a half-bodied person floating on a cloud of phosphorescence. Besides that, the crown of my head had started to shine with little dots of light. He also discovered that my arms had become extremely strong and powerful. Maybe it was the result my pushing the wheelchair. Thus I float and swim freely in and around the house. I feel completely satisfied and comfortable. The only trouble is that I can't help feeling sorry for my husband because all the household chores have become his burden. But I don't take this seriously once I see his happy-go-lucky attitude. At the beginning my children complained, but before long they got used to the fact and conscientiously shared part of the chores. Because I am very satisfied with my present situation, they feel that it is very natural for me to be sitting in the wheelchair. What outstanding children they are.

I remember the way my younger son explained the thing once when he came home from school. He said, "Somebody told me that you will die once you get wet from the rain. So don't go out for too long. It's dangerous."

"Who told you that? Who's poking his nose into my business?"

My son kept silent. He simply wouldn't tell me despite my pursuit. I started to feel uneasy. Instinct told me there was some kind of disgusting secret in my son's statement. Who was the person who couldn't wait to destroy my peaceful mind? Who on earth was my most direct enemy?

Suddenly it dawned on me: Could it be the spirit of my father-in-law that refuses to let go? After much thought he seemed to be the only one who could be considered an enemy. I told my husband about my uneasiness.

He replied, while glancing at our younger son with contempt and disapproval, "Don't even bother about the child's words. Pure nonsense. What's more, you can even order your legs to disappear from vision. This is some unusual ability that nobody can compete with. You should at least have that much confidence, huh?"

After listening to him I felt not only uneasy but also guilty. My uneasiness did not disappear.

After several days, my youngest son said to me again, "Mom, aren't you moving too much? You should pause for a while and think about something, somebody told me."

"But who?!" I blew up. In that instant, I found that all the phosphorescence on my body disappeared and both legs started to tremble.

"I can't tell . . ."

"Tell me immediately!"

". . . Grandpa."

"Hah! Where is he now?" I jumped up from the wheelchair, staggered toward my youngest son and caught his shoulder. I saw his face turn extremely pale and his eyes open wide as if he had seen a ghost.

"In his home! At his home! Everybody knows, except you!" My son started to sob. Covering his face with his hands, he ran away.

Hearing the sound, my husband rushed in and complained loudly, "Why do you bother? It would be so good if you just considered that old guy as dead! Yes, it's true that he recovered, but to us he's dead. That's why I told you he died. We have nothing to do with him."

"So he's not dead!" I howled like a lioness. I added, "I'm going back to my sports team and start my training."

"Aiya! Why bother about training? Why take the trouble? A person like you is simply unsuitable for running the marathon. I say it's a waste of energy. There are enough marathon champions. But how many can you find who are confined to a wheelchair by their own psychosomatic will? You should forget about the drawbacks. Just think about the advantages of your present life. Doesn't your food taste better this way?"

My husband's words are always very convincing. After a long silence I decided to accept his opinion because my experience tells me that it's always the most comfortable to deal with people and the world according to his opinion.

From that time on my legs have no longer been paralyzed, nor do they shine. They are no more than two normal legs. However, I still prefer sitting in a wheelchair without moving my legs, pushing the wheels with my hands instead. Such a life has brought me extreme inner peace.

My children are as busy as before. On the sly, they go to visit their grandpa. My husband still stands by me. But I no longer bother about those things. After a while I forgot everything about the past.

It's not until today, after so many years, when my youngest

son has brought the news that his grandpa's dead, that I re-member he had such a grandpa.

"On his deathbed he kept rumbling, 'Oh how lonely, how lonely.'"

My husband said, "Such people are born to suffer."

You see, my story ends like this.

THE
CHILD WHO RAISED
POISONOUS
SNAKES

Sha-yuan—one might call him Sandy Plain—was a child with an ordinary face, lacking any notable features. When he was not talking, his face was a dead blank. But of course this is somewhat different from being a corpse.

"He has been a well-behaved child," his mother explained to me. "The only trouble with him is that he should never be allowed outdoors. There wouldn't have been any trouble if he had stayed at home. We discovered his problem when he was only six. Once he sneaked away without the notice of his father and me. I looked for him everywhere. Finally we found him sleeping among the rosebushes in the park. He was lying on his back, with his limbs stretched out in a casual way. He told us later that he had not seen any roses, but many snake heads. He said he could even see the bones inside the snakes. Then, as one snake bit him, he had fallen asleep. To tell the truth, Sha-yuan hadn't seen a single snake in his life up to that point. He only saw snakes on TV. His father and I were terrified, and we were more cautious than ever not to let him out."

While we were talking, Sha-yuan was sitting in the room facing a cupboard door covered with paper resembling wood grain, absolutely still and motionless. In my astonishment, I kept peering at him.

"Don't pay any attention to him. He long ago acquired the ability not to listen whenever he doesn't want to. Once a doctor suggested that we take the child to a resort and let him socialize with other people. According to the doctor, this would improve his condition. So we went to the seashore. Sha-yuan often played with the kind of unruly children one finds at the seaside during the day. But he felt tired very easily. We had been observing him because we couldn't help feeling anxious about the child. Whenever he felt tired, he simply lay down no matter where and fell asleep. He became so languid that he could sleep while washing his feet in the evening. We thought he was washing, but it was no more than a mechanical movement—his brain was at rest.

"The third day after our arrival at the seaside, a fisherman's son ran in with a bleeding finger, telling us that Sha-yuan had bitten him. We questioned Sha-yuan afterward about the incident. He smiled absentmindedly and claimed that the finger was the head of a snake. If he had not bitten it, it would have bitten him. We stayed at the shore for a month. Apparently the beautiful scenery had no positive influence on Sha-yuan. That year he turned nine.

"After that, we traveled somewhere every year—to the desert or the lakes, to the forest or the plains. But Sha-yuan was completely indifferent. Sitting in the train, he behaved exactly as he did at home, never looking out the window, never talking to anybody. It was possible that he did not even know he was traveling. But his father and I knew that the child had been too carefree ever since he was young. He never paid attention to his surroundings. He might have been a little cold. I don't know how to put it, but he lacked sensitivity toward new things.

"It culminated last year when we discovered that his right arm was covered with wounds. Questioning him closely, we were led to a pitch-dark air-raid shelter where he squatted down with a flashlight. We found a box of little flowery snakes. His father asked him with horror where those snakes had come from. Sha-yuan replied: 'I caught them one after another.' This was very odd because he had been with us every day. Hadn't we watched him with care? 'I was not always with you. Don't be fooled by superficial appearances,' he said in his casual tone. After his father coaxed him away, I found a hoe and exterminated those little vipers.

"When we got home, we stayed up nights to prevent his sneaking away again. Yet after two days, fresh wounds had appeared on his arms—like pairs of red spots from snakebites. He said to us, 'Why bother to tire yourselves out. You simply can't understand that I'm only sitting with you in appearance. But there's no place I can't go even while I seem to be sitting with you. There are so many snakes, and they lose their way often. So I gather them from here and there, so they won't feel lonely. Of course you can't see them, but yesterday I found one over there under the bookshelf. I can always find snakes if

I look around. I was afraid of them when I was young. I even bit a snake's head once. I can't help laughing at myself when I think of it now.' He kept talking to us like this."

One day, while sitting with his back to us, Sha-yuan suddenly patted his head with his hand. We walked over, and Sha-yuan's mother turned him around so he was facing us. His facial expression was calm and relaxed. Cautiously choosing my words, I asked him what he was thinking about while sitting here, and if he was feeling lonely.

"Listen," he replied briefly.

"What do you hear?"

"Nothing, very quiet. But the situation will change completely after nine o'clock in the evening."

"How can you possibly dare to desert us like that? How can we live without you?" Sha-yuan's mother started her lament.

"You can't call it desertion," Sha-yuan said gently. "I was born to catch snakes."

I advised Sha-yuan's mother not to worry too much about her son. In my opinion, her boy, odd as he was, appeared to be a genius, who might one day turn out to be somebody.

"We don't care if he will be somebody," the mother said. "Both his father and I are only ordinary people. How is it that we should have a son who is involved in such shameful business? Raising poisonous snakes, that's frightening. What does he want to do? I might as well have given birth to a poisonous snake! We simply can't stop worrying about him. We're completely worn out by him. The worst thing is that now he can do strange things even without going outdoors. He always has a way to achieve what he wants."

One day I saw Sha-yuan's mother coming out of the air-raid shelter with a hoe in her hand. She looked wan and sallow. She told me she had just exterminated another nest of little snakes, eight altogether. She was almost bald, and she walked like an aged woman. Behind her appeared Sha-yuan's father, an old man who couldn't stop blinking one eye. Finally Sha-yuan himself emerged. His back was bent, and he appeared calm. When he saw me, he nodded and started talking: "I created this scene of slaughter on purpose. It might even be described as spectacular—eight lives destroyed once and for all. To them, it was not a matter of any particular terror. I was only surprised by the firmness and confidence of the hands that raised the hoe."

When asked if he was the one who took his parents to the shelter, he said yes. As soon as they asked, he took them there. He had always maintained a kind of curiosity about his parents' behavior. While he was talking, his mother stared at the sky with her empty eyes, and his father mumbled repeatedly: "Extreme views can cause tremendous difficulty in a person's life, but beautiful scenery can open one's mind."

I found that the slaughterer, the mother, was the most crestfallen among the three, but Sha-yuan remained detached. All at once it dawned on me that there existed a subtle relationship among these three, a peculiar mutual check. What had just happened was a proof. He didn't have to take his parents to the shelter; instead, he could have led them somewhere else. Was this only the result of his easygoing personality?

Then I recalled Sha-yuan's infancy. No doubt, he had been an extraordinarily sensitive baby, with extremely rich facial expressions. The mother had been very proud of him, yet she was nervous. She told me privately that she found the child got tired very easily, particularly when others were talking. As soon as a person started talking to him, he would lower his eyelids and fall into a sound sleep. "He's just like one of those sensitive mimosa plants whose leaves fold up when you touch them, though he's not as shy." Sha-yuan kept his habit until he was five. Then he learned to control himself, though purely for the sake of courtesy. When others talked to him a little bit too long, he would start yawning, then doze off without any consideration for the speaker.

At that time, he did not hate traveling. On the contrary, he appeared to like it somewhat, because he did not need to listen to others while traveling. While his parents were enjoying the beauty of nature, he would sit down to the side and listen attentively to any smallest sound made by little animals. He could always point out accurately where a field vole had just dug a hole, or in which direction a banded krait was advancing quietly. It was possible he had been training his unique listening ability ever since he was born. It seems, however, that this talent has never been tuned to the human voice. After several years' practice, he could make certain movements just by activating his mental will. On the surface, he was a soft and obedient kid. Such a child very easily makes people lose their vigilance. The fisherman's child was bitten under such circumstances. Now Sha-yuan's parents were getting hurt. It was a profound puzzle how he considered the people and objects surrounding him. On the one hand, he seemed to pity those little snakes, but on the other hand, he instigated his parents to slaughter them. Nobody can figure out such contradictory actions. I can't say that beautiful scenery did not affect him. It may have been the beautiful scenery that cultivated his temperament. After all, different people can appreciate scenery very differently. By the same token, his parents' painstaking efforts to control the child could only lead to the opposite result.

Then suddenly there came a day when Sha-yuan stopped meditating facing the wall, and his attitude toward his parents also turned warmer. Whenever I went for a visit, I always saw the threesome living in harmony. The smile had returned to his mother's face. In the past decade or so, the old lady had been completely tied down by her son. But now, even the wrinkles on her face had smoothed out. She said to me happily, "My child Sha-yuan is getting sensible. Just think how many poisonous snakes I have killed for his sake!" As she was talking, Sha-yuan in the background was nodding his head in agreement.

I did not believe the matter was as simple as that. I felt vaguely the falseness in Sha-yuan's smile. Though he was no longer raising poisonous snakes, who could guess what new trick he might be up to? I decided to talk to him seriously.

"Now I don't need a place to raise snakes," Sha-yuan answered. "They are in my belly. They don't stay inside all the time, of course. They come out whenever I want them to. The little flowery snake is my favorite."

Staring at his body, which was getting thinner daily, I asked if his mother knew about all of this. But Sha-yuan said that it was not necessary to let her know. Since the little snakes did not really occupy space, the matter need not be considered to exist so long as he did not mention it. Just let everybody be happy. My next question was whether this would affect his health.

He gave me an attentive look, then he suddenly appeared sleepy. Yawning hard, he said, "Who doesn't have something like that in his belly? They just don't know, that's all. That's why they're healthy. I'm always sleepy. You've talked so much. I rarely talk so much. You're weird."

Despite my efforts to ask for more, he dropped his head down and fell into a sound sleep while standing by the table.

Sha-yuan's mother got really excited, and she looked much younger now. While packing, she said, "It seems that travel is necessary." Sha-yuan joined her with joy in packing. But after a while, he turned aside and started vomiting. "Nothing serious." He wiped his pale lips and muttered almost secretly, "It was some mischief from the little flowery snake."

Quickly they started their journey on a northwest-bound train. It was a windy day.

They did not come back until two years later. The three

looked the same as they had been, harmonious and peaceful. Nothing unusual could be detected. Sha-yuan obviously had gained some weight, and his face looked healthier than before. When I asked him quietly about the snakes, he said they were still in his belly. But he had learned how to adjust, so that even running and doing the high jump would not cause him any harm. Sometimes, having snakes in his belly was even beneficial to his health. I asked him what benefit it could bring to the body, and Sha-yuan's yawns started again. He complained that it was painful to listen to others. Sha-yuan's mother invited me for dinner. While eating, the old lady, who used to grumble, was now silent. She did not appear as confident as before. Sha-yuan's father only said one sentence: "No more travel." Then everybody was quiet.

After that they kept their front gate open. The parents stopped watching Sha-yuan's behavior as if they had lost interest and become oblivious. But they appeared anxious and from morning till night they checked their watches constantly. Obviously they were waiting for something. "Waiting for their deaths," Sha-yuan said. He tapped his belly, which was flat. There was no sign of anything inside. According to Sha-yuan, it had worked out fine. Nobody suspected that he raised snakes anymore. But in fact, the leopard can't change its spots.

The fall wind was whistling across the plain. It sounded musical from morning to night. This mysterious family was baffling me more and more. I remembered that the mother was only fifty, and the father, fifty-five. But just see how old they looked. Both were suffering from cardiac arteriosclerosis and their slow movements worried me. "He has destroyed us," the father said suddenly one day. His facial expression revealed his confusion. "We are dying so fast." After the remark, his face relaxed instantly. His glance lingered on the skinny shoulder of Sha-yuan. The glance was both kind and loving. The three certainly had a tacit understanding.

The parents had different explanations about the disappearance of the child. According to the father, the boy had mentioned going to the air-raid shelter after supper, because he hadn't been there for a long time, and he was curious about any new changes there. Neither of the parents had paid any attention to their son's remark. They were too tired. The son then stood up and walked toward the door with staggering steps. Recently he had become all bony. He did not return that whole night, and nobody bothered looking for him. "It's too troublesome," the father said, his eyes fixed on the windowpane.

Sha-yuan's mother never admitted that her son had walked out on her. "The child was never reliable. For more than a decade, we had both kept our eyes wide open in watching, without any obvious effect. What can I say? He could still wander around at will without our seeing him. Now I've given up. Who knows whether or not he was my child to start with, or even if he had been living with us at all? I don't think he left yesterday. I've never even been able to confirm his existence."

Listening to them, I became perplexed also. What was Sha-yuan, after all? I pondered hard, but in my mind there

CHILD WHO RAISED POISONOUS SNAKES

were only some miscellaneous fragments, some odd remarks. When I tried to concentrate, even the remarks faded away. As a result, I could not think of anything about Sha-yuan except his name.

Just when everybody believed that he had vanished, however, Sha-yuan came back. He resumed his quiet and friendly life at home. His behavior once again contributed to the indifferent attitude of his parents. They no longer cared at all if the boy existed or not. They were simply worn out.

"Where did you get the name Sha-yuan?" I asked abruptly.

"I've been wondering about it myself. Nobody ever gave him that name. Where *did* it come from?" the mother said, looking confused.

HOMECOMING

As a matter of fact, I'm very familiar with this area. For some time I came here every day. However, now it's too dark, and the moon is reluctant to come out, so I can go forward only by instinct. After a while, I smell an odor. It's from a small chestnut tree. Past the chestnut tree, dry grass crackles under my step. Now I feel relaxed. Here's a stretch of grassland. No matter which direction you face, you can't reach the end of the prairie without at least half an hour's walk. The ground is very flat, without even any dips. Once my younger brother and I conducted an experiment here by walking forward for ten minutes with our eyes closed. We both came through the trial safe and sound.

Reaching the grassland, I wander about aimlessly. I know that soon afterward I'm going to see a house. Ultimately I will arrive there without having to give it much thought. In the past this method always brought me unexpected joy. Once I enter that house, I will sit down and drink a cup of tea with the owner (a pale-faced gentleman with no beard or hair). Then one breath will take you down along a zigzag mountain trail until you reach a grove of banana trees. The owner is rather kind, and, in his reluctance to part, always accompanies me to the corner, where I have to turn. He always wishes me good luck. The most comfortable thing is the downhill trail, which is very easy to walk. Soon there will appear a monkey to greet me. Each time I nod at him, and then he leads the way. Usually, when I reach the banana grove, I lie down beneath a tree and eat my fill. Then I go home. On my way home there is no monkey. Of course I never lose my way, because everything is so familiar to me. Strangely, the way home is again downhill, and I walk without any effort. Why is that? I've never understood the logic in this.

Wandering like this, I know I've reached the house because my forehead has suddenly bumped into the brick wall. Tonight the owner of the house hasn't put on the light. Nor does he greet me from the stoop as he usually does.

"Why should you come so late?" he says from inside the window. He sounds a bit unhappy. Feeling his way around for a long time, he opens the door with a creak.

"I can't turn on the light," he says. "It's too dangerous. I guess you still don't know that behind our house there is a deep abyss. This house was built on a cliff. I've been hiding this fact from you in the past, but I can't anymore. Do you remember that I always accompany you to the corner, chatting about something distracting? I was afraid that you might turn your head and see the position of the house!"

I sit down at the table.

"That's not too difficult," the owner continued. In the darkness he passes a cup of lukewarm water into my hand.

"Once in a while it comes out. I mean the moon. You can see it now. I really can't turn on the light. Please forgive me. This house has reached its dying age. Please listen, and you will understand everything."

What he's saying is patent nonsense. It's obvious to me that the house is situated at the end of the flat grassland with its back toward the mountain. I can remember clearly. Once I even circled around to the back of the house and fed pigeons there! But now he has made it so terrifying that I have to be more cautious.

In fact, the moon still hasn't come out, and there's no sound whatsoever from outside. It's a silent, suffocating night. It could be that the owner has lost his mind during my absence for all these years.

He sits quietly in front of me, smoking.

"Maybe you don't believe me. Just stand up and have a look!"

Supporting myself with the table, I stand up. All of a sudden I fall forward onto the ground without anybody pulling me.

"Now you understand." I suppose he is smiling slightly. "It's terrible, such a thing. Light is absolutely forbidden. And the banana grove can be reached only under the condition that you do not turn your head and look back. Well, my little deceptions are something from the past. Maybe you won't even care about them anymore."

"Now I have to wait until morning to leave." I sigh and say, "When the dawn comes I'll be able to see and it will be convenient for me to go."

"You're completely wrong," he says, deep in thought while smoking. "There won't even be a question of dawn. I've told you that the house has reached its dying age. Can't you imagine what's left? Since you have forced your way in, I have to arrange a room for you. Of course, the light cannot be turned on. You'd better calm yourself down and listen. You can hear how those sea waves are striking against the cliff."

Of course I can't hear anything. Outside the window appears a dark shadow that might be the mountain. I remember this house is located at the foot of a mountain. I listen intently. Still there is dead silence.

"How can the dawn come?" The owner has guessed what I'm thinking. "You will understand. As time goes by, you will understand everything. Once you force your way in, you have to live here. It's true, you've been here in the past, and every time I saw you off in person. But then you were only passing through—that's not the same thing as forcing your way in. Then this house was not as old as it is now."

I mean to argue, I mean to tell him that I did not intend to force my way in. As in the past, I am, again, just passing through. I would not have come if I had known that my behavior constituted "forcing my way in." But I open my mouth without saying anything, as if I am too timid and ashamed.

"The foundation of the house is very fragile, and it's built on top of the cliff. Right behind the house there's a deep abyss. You should be aware of this situation. Now that you're here, you can live in a small room on the right. Actually, I am not the owner of this house. The original owner has departed. I, too, came here by accident, and I stayed. At that time the original owner was not very old. One day he went to the back of the house to feed the pigeons. When I heard a sound, I went out back, but I couldn't find him. He had disappeared. That was when I discovered the cliff behind the house. Of course the original owner had jumped over the edge. I never had a chance to ask him why he had built the house in such a place. I still find it puzzling. But I've gotten used to the idea."

He leads me to the appointed small room and orders me to lie down on the wooden bed. He tells me not to think about anything, explaining that this way I can hear what's happening outside. And he tells me not to expect the dawn, that such a thing does not even exist anymore. I have to learn to adjust to this new environment in which I must depend on the senses of touch and hearing. As silently as a fish he leaves me. For a long, long time I am in doubt as to whether he is exaggerating. For example, he considers my coming here as "forcing my way in," and he makes much of the cliff and the abyss. But what do these have to do with putting on a light?

I don't know how long I've been sleeping in silence. Finally I've made up my mind. I find a lighter in my pocket and start a small fire. In that faint light I search the small room up and down without finding anything. It's an extremely ordinary room. The ceiling is made of bamboo strips. The only furniture in the room is the old wooden bed that I have lain on. On the bed there's a cotton mattress and a quilt. There is perfect silence, and there appear to be no terrible changes in the house because of the light I am making. Obviously the owner of the house is exaggerating. Maybe he's suffering from some neurosis. A lot of things in the world are hard to figure. These are all kinds of possibilities. To be cautious, I had better keep still. Besides, there isn't much fluid left in my lighter. I should save it. It's the same as the blindfold game I used to play with my younger brother. We would limit our travel to only ten minutes. The whole situation might have turned out completely differently if we had set our time limit at one hour. Furthermore, what is the structure of the human ears? For example, can my ears stay this quiet forever? As for the owner of the house, can he find a way to keep himself alert? How can he be so listless for such a long time?

I hear him coming. Feeling around, he says, "So, one corner of the ceiling has dropped! Those explosions just now were horrifying. I hope you didn't make any light. In the waves below, a fishing boat is sinking. I suspect the fisherman on the boat is the original owner of this house. Such things always seem to have a relationship to each other. According to the account I've heard, the fishing boat has run aground on the rocks. The whole boat is smashed to bits and the dead man is lying peacefully amidst the seaweed. Above him is the little house he built with his own hands. . . . Of course this story is pure nonsense. How can he see any house? He's choked to death on seawater. And there's nothing poetic about it at all. He's lying at the bottom of the sea, his face down, buried in the sand and stone. He will rot, gradually. . . . Now I'm returning to my room. You should just calm down and stay here. Gradually you'll find that everything is fine. Certainly better than your wandering all over the place."

I try to walk out of the house. The earth is trembling terribly. Clinging to the ground, I crawl outside the front gate. In front of me should be the flat stretch of grassland. As soon as I stand up and walk, I feel suddenly that it's not grass under my feet but something hard and moving. I start to change direction. But no matter which direction I walk I can never reach the grassland, and beneath my feet there's always that lump of moving substance. Surrounding me is a stretch of grayish black. Except for the vague silhouette of the house, I can't even see the mountains. Of course, I can't go behind the house. According to the owner, there's a cliff. Since I have walked randomly along the grassland, I should be able to walk back as long as I walk randomly. There's no need to feel tense. With these thoughts in mind, I start walking randomly in some direction. In the beginning nothing happens. I start to feel a little bit pleased with myself. About a hundred paces on, I suddenly step into empty air. Fortunately, I get caught in a little tree sticking out and I climb back onto the cliff. I remember very well that I started walking from the front of the house. Why have I reached the cliff? Does that mean that "different roads lead to the same destination"? Where's the trail through the grassland? I ponder hard. It seems there should be some answer. In fact, I have vaguely felt that answer for a long time, but subconsciously I have refused to recognize it. Clutching the ground, I crawl back into the house. Inside, there's a kind of relaxation and a safe feeling. I even feel that the darkness and the smell of the lime are familiar, cozy, comfortable. In the darkness, the owner of the house hands me a cup of water—lukewarm and with a smell of being unboiled, but it's still drinkable.

"I have to say something," the owner of the house announces. At that moment I smell the fragrance of a cigarette. "It's about him. He wears a black garment and a black hat. Even his leg wrappings are black. He appeared on the street of the town as if he were an ancient bandit. Some people passed right in front of him without even noticing him. Others spied on him secretly from those shuttered windows. Both sides of the street were completely lined with barbershops. Inside sat many customers waiting to have their hair cut. Some of them appeared to be in high spirits. Nobody knew where all the barbers had gone. The customers did not notice the black-clothed person. Those who spied on him behind the windows were all pedestrians who had noticed him and had sneaked into the barbershops quickly, hiding themselves behind the curtains. The sun was burning, and he was soaked with sweat. Stretching his arms, he appeared to be driving something away. Those who were hidden observed, with pale faces, the performance of that black-jacketed man. Without anybody pushing him, he fell down. A large number of people swarmed out and circled him.

"'Send him home!' ordered one of those who had been hidden.

"'Right! Send him home!' all those that surrounded him agreed.

"Just don't think about things like the dawn. Then you can harmonize yourself with the house. The sky will never lighten. Once you keep this rule in mind, you will feel comfortable. It's because he was too listless that the original owner jumped into the sea from the cliff behind the house and became a fisherman. Every day I listen here, and I can always hear him struggling in the stormy sea. You and I do not belong to the sea below, we two. You knew the answer long ago. The original owner's skill as a sailor was not very good. He was good at building a house. Therefore, his boat running into the rocks is unavoidable."

Quietly he returns to his own room.

As soon as I heard the owner telling me that below the cliff is the sea, I started to feel an irrational attraction to that imaginary world below. I don't know how long I've been staying in this house. I can't keep track because I don't have my watch with me and it's always so dark. Also, my lighter has long since run out of fluid. Whenever I feel bored, I chat with the owner about the sea. And every time, he hands me a cup of lukewarm water and smokes his cigarette. He always starts the conversation with this sentence: "The little boat of the original owner has arrived . . ." Every time, I object: "But the original owner is dead, isn't he? He ran his boat onto the rocks." At that moment he smiles, and the red glow of his cigarette flashes. Paying no attention to my objection, he continues this talk: "Upon its departure I went to see the boat off. On the boat there was only one fisherman. I heard that he died of old age later on. Then the owner himself became the fisherman. He never fished. Instead he only picked up seaweed and such things to fill his stomach. Afterward his face gradually turned blue."

With some understanding, I say, "We two are living above. We never turn on the light. So it's almost as if we don't exist, isn't that so? Even if the original owner passed by below, he would never notice the house above him. It's very possible that he once mistook this lump of black shadow as a tree. Calmly he must have glanced at it and immediately turned his glance away."

After a while, without knowing it, I join the discussion. We talk so eagerly that we feel uncomfortable when we lapse into silence. But once we say something, we immediately feel that we are too talkative. Time passes like this. Of course, there is no clock, and the dawn never comes. The owner of the house says that before long I will be acclimated to the fact that there is no seasonal change. He also says we cannot use the content of our talk as the basis to sort out the years, months, or days because we forget completely about our talks the next day. Besides, the little boat itself is fictitious and it's meaningless except for filling our need to divert ourselves from boredom.

When we feel tired from talking, we doze off separately. Upon waking, I remember fragments of what happened in the past. I remember that I found that trail from the very beginning, the single little trail toward the grassland. Although I have walked on that trail hundreds of times, I still have to look for it every time, though I never put much effort into looking for it. But what happened next is vague. It seemed that a flamingo was chasing me desperately. I was not afraid of it, yet he could never catch up to me. He ran always in the same position, as if held in place by a magnetic stone. I'm wondering if the small trail that I have used hundreds of times is really the only way to reach here. Since in my original memory this house is located at the end of a stretch of grassland with its back toward the mountain, there should be several ways, from several different directions, to reach here. For example, one could come down from the mountain, or from the south or west of the grassland. Who's to say that there's no path in those places? Once in the dim light I really saw a human figure in the west and I believe I was not mistaken. Would the flamingo come again?

But now the owner of the house firmly eliminates all the possibilities. He insists that there is a deep abyss behind the house, and that there has never been grassland in front of the house—just the rolling sand and stones. But how did I come here? According to him, this was only a chance incident. The so-called grassland and the banana groves are nothing but illusions that I made for myself. At the beginning there was a trail behind the house, the trail where he saw me off. But after several big explosions the trail has been blocked by mud and sand. The original owner of the house had calculated the odds before he chose this location to build his house. It is usual for people to pass by this location accidentally. In the past, many people have passed by the house by chance as I did. He received them politely and saw them off at the corner. Nobody noticed anything abnormal. But my forcing my way in this time was something unexpected. That was why he was a little bit upset at the beginning, though now he feels okay.

I insist on looking at the pigeons at the back of the house. I say that we should feed the little creatures. With a sneer, he agrees reluctantly. But he says we'll have to go through the tunnel in the kitchen to get to the cliff at the back of the house. In such a place it is enough for a person to stretch out her head and have a glance. He can't imagine why I have the idea that there would be pigeons in such a place. Besides, how could I ever get to the kitchen? I might entertain such fantasies, but once I tried to actually move, I would fall to the ground.

Although I am living in a room apart from the owner's, his existence is a comfort for me. My skeptical mind has gradually calmed down. Every time I awake I hear the owner's greeting: "So, you're up." In the darkness I put on my clothes and then sit in the living room with the owner every day without exception. When we have nothing to talk about, we sit in silence. I don't feel particularly listless, just a little bit bored.

AN
EPISODE WITH
NO FOUNDATION

There's one kind of guard that can hardly be called a guard. Those who belong to this category do nothing but sit at the foot of the bare mountains, month after month, year after year, until they forget their own existence. In the silence, the sound of a branch can be heard, broken by the wind, knocking against the trunk, one blow after another. I call such people guards. Why? Maybe I'm using the term as an excuse to fill the utter emptiness in my own heart, or maybe I consider it a real explanation."

"No, there's nothing that can be named that needs to be guarded. As soon as I open my mouth, I feel superficial and frivolous. Nevertheless, there's always a mountain behind you, and there's the resonance of a branch striking. Sitting there, you listen attentively, all alone. This is contradictory to common sense. In the morning, when the sun rises, the world becomes noisy. Yet you sleep in the sunshine, completely oblivious to the surroundings. This is another contradiction of common sense.

"There are always two or three people listening at the feet of different mountains. Nobody is aware of their existence. Even they themselves can't figure out the puzzle: How did this person arrive at the mountain? How did his person sit down under a tree and never move again? Did anybody look for this person when he or she disappeared from the crowd? Could it be that one of the relatives stamped his foot and discovered certain traces of the person? Does such a disappearance last forever? Is there a possibility of the person's return?

"I think you are guarding because you have been sitting in the same place without any movement and because you have always heard the sound. Few people have mentioned the significance of such work, but rather have relegated it to the category of insignificant work. Ordinary people would consider it unnecessary. As I happen to know, there's another person doing the same thing in a place quite a distance from here. He is completely ignorant of your situation, and he has also disappeared from the crowd unintentionally. At one moment, he was bending over to take off his shoes in order to dump out the sand and dirt. All of a sudden, people realized he had disappeared. His family members called his name loudly.

"You should think this way: There exist in this world two people who are listening to the sound of a branch striking the trunk in two different places. These two are very much alike. You may think that I am telling a lie, but your doubt is unimportant. The important thing is that it is a fact—you are listening all the time."

"I've forgotten the details of how I disappeared, and of other things as well. For instance, am I still a youngster or a dying old man? As a result of sitting here for so long, I can't make such judgments anymore. I only remember vaguely that there was a time when the wind was fairly strong, and that is when the branch was broken. Now the wind has died down, though there is hardly a chance for complete quiet.

"To tell you the truth, I've been assuming there is someone else doing the same thing somewhere else. Without such an assumption, I would keep silent with the mountain and stop listening to any sound. There is such a possibility. Can an assumption last forever? Would I still be able to hear the monotonous sound of the striking once this assumption disappears?"

"Of course you may call your present condition an illusion. As a matter of fact, the other person has been on guard at his location the whole time. I can see him whenever I want to. He never talks, never makes any sound. Yet he is there. You two who have disappeared will never meet each other. You carry on a silent dialogue through me, you realize each other's existence through me. Now you should feel satisfied.

"Let me tell you your age—you are neither young nor old. This question doesn't require consideration, because the physical changes in your body have long been at a standstill.

"Just think, he did nothing but bend over to take off his shoes—such a trivial event. Nobody had anticipated his disappearance. Such things are always somewhat mysterious. If I tell them that he is sitting at a place not very far from where they are, and that a careful search might result in some discovery, they would give me a cold stare and keep silent with their heads bowed low. Among them there was one young fellow who told me once that he really shouldn't have left. They had many foresters, and there was no need for him to take the job. Besides, guarding a forest was a job suitable only for the elderly, and he was still a youngster."

"I once admired the forester, one who has a substantial mind and a definite goal. But now I can see how laughable the idea is. There are also fishermen and hunters who are clear-headed, vigilant, and courageous. Do I envy them because I have nothing to guard or kill? I'm doing nothing but sitting at the foot of this bare mountain, addlepated and half asleep. Whenever the moon is covered by the clouds, I can't even feel my own existence."

"You are only sitting here. There are two people doing the same thing.

"And I am taking the responsibility of a messenger. Now let me confess to you that I was born a messenger. Just now I've told you about the event of his bending down to take off his shoes. You should have made all kinds of associations. I always convey such information to people like you, and sincerely enjoy doing it. Before my arrival, you had only an assumption about the existence of the other person. And you are often doubtful of such assumptions. Now I have proved your assumption. That is my specialty. I have a unique ability—I can see anything if I want. Such an ability is very beneficial in a messenger."

"If the person who has captured and killed the lion finally becomes the prey of the lion, at the instant of death, what kind of information would be transmitted from deep inside his pupils?"

"Yes, I've seen eyes like that—they're monochromatic, and they are completely different from the eyes of guards like you. When you are listening attentively to the sound of the branch striking, your eyes are simply blazing with colors. It's a pity that you can't see the color yourself, a real pity. We always have many things that we feel pity about. It doesn't matter whether we can make sense of it or not. Just quit making sense. Making sense is too troublesome. You have certainly quit thinking of such troublesome things long ago."

"I must have been sitting here for a long time, yet I've never had one dream! I've forgotten how to dream. I tried and tried, but in vain—either I can't go to sleep at all, or I sleep like a log without any dreams. Why are such things so easy to forget? I would go to sleep while thinking about that branch, hoping the branch would enter my dreamland. But once I fall into sleep, everything turns black. It seems that I am too single-minded—one dark tunnel to the bottom. Now I'm not able to see anything once I fall asleep."

"Such an ending is unchangeable. Both of you sleep amidst darkness. You look and look but can see nothing. It's no use to struggle. Some people are so extremely upset that they end their lives early for it. But I can see you are nothing of that kind. You close your eyes in time and fall into sleep.

"It happened that before you arrived here, all the dreams had been dreamed, and you had entered a dreamless territory. Fortunately I can tell you how magnificently colorful the light from your eyes is. It is through me, the messenger, that you have found out that fact. I'll convey such information to you frequently. It's my privilege as well as yours. Once you enter the dreamless territory, you have obtained this privilege permanently.

"There are very few pure guards. Once they appear, messengers like me occur with them. Only once in a while does this world produce guards like you and messengers like me. We are rare, and nobody cares for us. Sometimes the world simply stops producing people like us. As a result, the world is flooded with foresters everywhere."

"I really need the comfort you bring me. The first time I received it, I was totally infatuated with it. But now I've gotten used to it, and am not that excited. When I feel idle, I recall the experience you described to me—because it is somewhat strange that eyes can beam out a variety of colors. This reminds me of the old puzzle: Would my eyes keep beaming out that strange light without the existence of you, the messenger? Is it because of the special structure of your eyes that you can receive the information from my eyes? This puzzle has always added a layer of shadow to the comfort I receive.

"Another problem is that my eyes and ears are losing their functions gradually because I sleep during the day. Consequently many colors and shapes and many words are disappearing from my memory. At this moment I am searching carefully. In my mind there appear only two words, 'mountain' and 'tree.' Yet when I pronounce these two words, the corresponding images do not appear.

"As I'm sitting here, I sometimes work out something completely unfamiliar in my mind. For instance, I imagined that a magnificent gathering was once held right here. Among the participants were numerous strangers. When the gathering ended, people gradually left, some running toward the street for the bus, some taking shortcuts home. The ground was littered with scraps of paper. As for me, it seems that I did attend the gathering, and I stayed on after the meeting. It was just before dawn and dew was about to fall. The last person left on a bicycle. He even rang his bike bell. With my back against a rock, I fell into a confused sleep. Until that point, I hadn't had a thought about becoming a guard. I only felt tired and needed to rest by the rock. I was confident that I would go home eventually. I even determined the direction I would be heading. But afterward I felt apathetic about returning home.

"I also imagined that on the path to the country I met a man in a dark green robe. I brushed his shoulder as we passed each other. I couldn't help turning to look back—only to find that he was walking hurriedly. Consequently, I hastened my pace in the opposite direction. That was how I arrived at the foot of this mountain. He could have been the person you mentioned, or he might not be that man at all. During the first few days after my arrival, I could vaguely recognize the path that had led me here, because I had made signs at every bend and fork. But now that path no longer exists."

"I'm the only one who knows exactly how you disappeared. But I'll never tell you. I can only tell it to the other person, the one who is sitting at the foot of the mountain, as you are. And I can only tell you about him, but not the person himself. The distance between you two is somewhat wide, so wide that you will never be able to meet. Thus the stories of your own disappearances will remain secrets from each of you.

Therefore, you will continue using your imagination to pass the endless time.

"If you like, you may consider me as a bird flying between you and the other person. You will imagine forever. Both of you have once lived among crowds of people, and therefore both have learned about logic and imagination. The game is pretty simple, yet effective. But I'm only an observer. In the shadows of the mountain, the eternal light is pulsating. And I have become the only witness of the spectacle.

"Your ears are just suitable for listening to that sound; your eyes started shining as soon as you arrived here. As a result, you've forgotten the past. However, I remember everything, but I'm not going to tell you. No matter if you ask me or not, I'll tell you some anecdotes about the other person; for one example, how he bent to pour the sand and dirt out of his shoes, and how he disappeared right after that. For another example, he seems to have a brother who left home with him that day. After the disappearance, the young man's shrill voice stood our amidst those calling for the vanished one. However, the person who disappeared did not hear anything. He walked very fast. What he did could be described either as duty-bound and regret-free, or as hasty action. At the corner, he kicked off his shoes. Barefooted he arrived at the foot of the mountain, and fell down in a sleep."

This imaginary dialogue could probably go on forever. But if you watch the two speakers carefully, you will realize that their lips have never moved. The dialogue recorded above is merely an episode that the author has written down without any foundation. Many things can never be decided, and many people's lives have been wasted in trying to solve unresolvable puzzles. But the mountain remains silent.

As for those people who have voluntarily disappeared, what have they been thinking? It seems nobody will ever know, and the author can only imagine, on and on.

Why didn't anybody at that kind of grand gathering near the river notice that a person was about to disappear forever? I have heard that such occurrences happen very rarely, yet the relatives of the vanished person never search for long. They gather at the riverbank and call out loudly until exhausted and then return home the very next dawn. The second night, they call at the riverbank again. But the number shrinks sharply and only a few show up. After the third day, nobody goes back to the riverbank, but instead everybody discusses the odd event at home. By the turn of the new year, nobody raises the issue anymore, as if everybody had agreed beforehand to fall silent. The clothing of the vanished person would still be kept in the wardrobe. His bowl and chopsticks would still be placed on the table at mealtime. The family members would pretend that he still lived with them in the house.

I once visited the relative of a vanished person. This relative was a tragic character with long hair and beard and an expressionless face. Yet his hands were restless with anxiety. One after another, he tore the buttons off his jacket. He repeated, "It was completely unnecessary to take such extreme action." His tone sounded quite superficial. I asked him to talk about what happened that night. "I bid him goodnight, not having the faintest idea that he would leave. Isn't that funny?" That was all he could remember.

I strolled to the riverbank and looked around. I found a horse galloping against the wind, and the dead rider had a secretive expression on his face.

A

DREAMLAND

NEVER DESCRIBED

The Recorder sat in his roadside shed writing down the various dreamlands described by passersby. This had gone on for many years, and he had recorded a nearly infinite variety of images. Usually a session went like this: the passersby—all ordinary people who appeared a bit confused as they entered the shed—walked in and sat down on the floor. Their descriptions differed from person to person and ranged from vivid to dull and mechanical, confusingly meditative, or obscure. The Recorder sat before them, showing no facial expression. He copied verbatim, collecting everything into a black notebook. Then the passersby would leave, sullenly.

Gradually the number of people with dreams to report decreased, and the Recorder felt more and more lonely, yet he continually stretched his neck out stubbornly and stared toward the end of the road. He was hoping for a dreamland that had never yet been described, one charged with heat and blinding light. He was not even sure what he had imagined in his own mind. But he believed firmly there was such a dreamland. Yet he could not by himself write this dreamland directly into the black notebook; he had to wait for someone to come in who could set it forth as it had appeared in his own dream. That person would describe this dream to the Recorder in the shed by the roadside, and the Recorder would copy it down for him. Because existence travels in zigzag paths, all the Recorder could do was wait.

Day after day, the people who arrived could never describe directly the image in the Recorder's mind; therefore, this image could never be turned into words, and its authenticity could never be established. As a result, the Recorder became disheartened day by day, yet he still stretched out his neck stubbornly. His hands and feet cracked in the bitter wind of winter, and in the dampness of spring his joints swelled like little steambuns. In addition, the run-down shed by the roadside started leaking. Most passersby no longer stopped to describe their dreamlands; instead they flung cold glances in his direction and continued on their way. The Recorder observed every one of them carefully, and his heart pulsed regularly between hope and disappointment. Sometimes a whole day would pass with only one or two people coming into his shed. And their dreamlands were nothing out of the ordinary, although they were filled with the mad joy of wandering in the vast universe; or with the conceitedness of a person who locks himself inside a cave deep within the shell of the earth; or with the horror of being captured by some beast of prey; or with the ghastly feeling of being in the process of dying. However, no one ever dreamed the image that appeared in the Recorder's mind.

Maybe this was nothing but a kind of torture. The Recorder had asked himself this question numerous times, and numerous times had failed to find the answer. But just at the moment when the passersby with dreams were leaving, the light of that dreamland that had never been described would make his body tremble all over. This trembling—the trembling itself—confirmed in him the existence of that image. So he named that image that had never been described nor had ever occurred clearly in his mind "the wind." "The wind" always arose when the person with dreams was leaving. Now what he was expecting with his stretched-out neck was more than merely the dreamers. When they were leaving, he knew, that light would appear. He had begun to see this more and more clearly.

Then in the rainy season there came an old woman holding a huge umbrella. Her snow-white hair had been tousled by the wind. The eyeballs inside their deep, narrow sockets had no vision, yet she was not blind. She entered the shed and let the Recorder touch her ice-cold fingers, then she went on her way. It was on that day that the Recorder stopped writing down the descriptions of the dreamlands of the passersby. Nor did he stare down the road anymore. He was still waiting, however, and he seemed to know what he was waiting for. With the passing of time, that image of his had changed gradually into something less definite, and his hearing deteriorated daily. Very often when a passerby entered the shed, the Recorder was still in his reverie. Only one thing was clear: at a certain moment his heart would throb in response to that invisible light and that empty image, and his blood would surge like a herd of running horses.

Once in a while there were still people stopping by his shed. The dreamlands they described had become more and more outrageous. Each one complained that the thing he had seen was indescribable. And because it was indescribable, they sometimes left, disheartened, in the middle of their account. The Recorder, understanding all this, held his black notebook and pen in his hands and pretended to be listening carefully. As a matter of fact, he did not record anything. When the person with the dream left, in his mind's eye there still appeared the image that once had made him tremble, yet it had faded into a blankness with something like shadows swaying back and forth within it. He couldn't confirm this, yet he was satisfied. Closing his notebook he sat on the floor for a break, and the instant of the break was sweet.

The following is a dialogue between the Recorder and a person reporting a dream:

DREAMER: What have I been talking about? What I have said is not even as much as one tenth of what I saw. That feeling could never occur again. Why can't I describe it? It's so disheartening! The wind is too strong here.

RECORDER: Uh-huh.

DREAMER: Whatever you have recorded here is all rubbish. Yet we still come to you because everybody knows you are the only person who records

those things here. I really want to describe it. Please
tell me—is it because I am not verbal?
RECORDER: What you've said is really interesting.

After the dreamers left, they never revealed to others the
image that they had described to the Recorder, as if there were
an unspoken agreement among them. After they had described their dreamlands to him, they felt they had left a piece
of valuable property in his run-down shed. As a matter of
fact, they seldom reflected on what they had described, yet
they remembered making the description because that was
their property. They paid no attention to whether or not the
recorder had written anything in his notebook. What they
did pay attention to was the very act of describing inside the
shed. Although during their descriptions they were also continually grumbling and complaining, as if impatient or totally
bored, deep inside they were quite satisfied with themselves.
Once they left that shed they felt they became mere ordinary
people. They tended to consider the unique communication
between themselves and the Recorder as a supreme secret.
They also tended to see that black notebook as something
that made them feel intimate and commited to something in
their hearts.

Nobody had expected that the Recorder would abandon
his black notebook, because it contained such a quantity of
unique and strange dream images, and it was therefore considered by many people as the property of the many dreamers.
But now he had thrown the notebook away, and he explained

this only indifferently: "It flew away without wings." And he refused to raise the issue again.

Random passersby continued to enter his run-down shed. As usual he sat on the floor, straight and solemn, listening to their descriptions without making a sound himself. The disappearance of the notebook hadn't affected the unique communication between them. Among those random passersby were some who had visited him before and others who had never been there. Without mentioning it, they all experienced the benefit of not having the notebook because now they could talk about whatever they wanted without worrying. After they had arrived at the Recorder's shed, every one of them would speak, whether for a long time or a short time. So they started talking, yet who could hear clearly what they were talking about? That was impossible. It was not until today— this is quite a few years after it happened—that we realized that those people had never said anything meaningful. Instead they were only pronouncing some syllables willy-nilly to pass the time. And the Recorder was not listening carefully but only pretended to pay attention. As a matter of fact, he was thinking of something else. It was certain that he was thinking of that blank image and waiting impatiently for its arrival. Yet he knew that one cannot rush this sort of thing. Therefore, he had to pretend to be listening to the dreams. It was with such purposeful procrastination that they passed the endless time, repeating the same thing again and again, patiently.

From the Recorder's point of view, throwing away the notebook was, of course, perfect. Though it did have some drawbacks, however, one being that he was now more and more dependent on the dreamers. He had classified his life into several periods, according to the kind of dreamers who arrived. He no longer remembered how much time he had spent in the shed. In fact, his concept of time had completely disappeared. Whenever he was recalling certain events, he would think this way: "That's the day when that dark, skinny-faced man arrived . . ." or "That afternoon when the woman with butterfly freckles arrived . . ." "That day when nobody stopped by . . ." or "That morning when the person came, then left without saying anything . . ." et cetera. Such classifications appeared very convenient, yet because fewer people were coming to him lately, his memory was deteriorating. This method of classification, as a result, embodied great vagueness and even error because it distorted sequence, and very often uncertainty would creep in. Fortunately, now he didn't care that much about such things, and he had become increasingly casual.

If on one day more than two dreamers arrived, the Recorder would regard that day as a festival. When they had departed, he would still sit in the shed with his straight back and with his solemn expression. His whole body, including his heart, was trembling amidst the light that nobody, not even he himself, could see. Such an event was not common, and the Recorder knew it himself; therefore, he didn't appear anxious. He also knew that the dreamers did not come of their own free will. The will that determined their arrival was in fact inside his mind. Now that he had stopped stretching out his neck to stare down the road, most of the time he felt calm.

His only hint of impatience would occur at the moment when a dreamer arrived, because he already knew what the consequence would be. Afterward, he could be seen creeping about, shivering in the cold wind and blowing warm air onto his fingers, which were as swollen at the joints as little steamed buns, yet in his eyes there danced indescribable ecstasy.

Many people say that the Recorder was a fictitious being because he couldn't even prove his own existence, and they are right. There was no proof of the existence of the Recorder himself, at least for the middle and late periods of his career in recording. He was shrinking into his strange and unique shell, until finally nobody could see any trace of him. What they saw was only an empty shell that had been abandoned by the roadside. The shell was similar to the most ordinary shell of the river clam. Once in a while someone asserted that he could hear the sound of the Recorder as though from an extremely deep rock cave, but because that cave was so profound, when the sound reached his ear it was almost like the weeping of an ant. Such assertions were of little value.

It's true that every day we saw the Recorder sitting in the shed by the road in the same posture and behaving in the same way. The strange thing was that whenever we thought of him as being a member of our own species, there would arise unexpected doubts about his personal life, as well as that mysterious communication between him and the dreamers. But these were things that had been explained from his own personal perspective. Without that, everybody felt it would be impossible to make an adequate analysis of him. Almost nobody could remember any specific details about him, such as a word or phrase, a facial expression, a gesture, a line he had written, and so on. Everything about him existed in his own description, yet that description was only dimly discernible and lacked continuity. The key here was that others could not re-create him, describe him, in their own words.

Nineteen-ninety was the tenth year after the Recorder set up his shed by the roadside. There was an unparalleled snowstorm. After the big snow, all the inhabitants swarmed into the streets, stamping their feet and blowing warm breath into their hands while they discussed the storm. When they walked into the run-down shed of the Recorder, they saw that the storm had blown away half of the roof, and inside the snow was piled up more than two feet deep. People found the Recorder sitting quietly in the snowdrifts. His eyebrows and hair were piled with snowflakes. No one noticed that a column of steam was rising from the back of his neck. What kind of energy source was burning inside his body?

"From now on no one will come to discuss their dreamlands," the Recorder declared to the arrivals in a firm tone. "That era has passed. I have decided this just now." Nobody was listening to him. Nobody was noticing him. Nobody had ever thought of noticing him.

The Recorder was still sitting by the roadside waiting. Now there was no longer anybody to come to him. That is to say, what he was waiting for was no longer those dreamers. His body was seated straight. His dried, skinny face was always inclined toward the north, and on his face there was an expression of having abandoned everything. He was still indulging himself in that empty image, yet people could no longer discern his reaction toward it. What people saw was a person in rags, perhaps an idiot, wasting time, sitting in a tumbledown shed by the roadside. Such unconventional behavior did not arouse people's good feeling toward him; instead, now people snubbed him. When they were passing by, they would turn their heads away intentionally, or they would raise their voices, pretending not to notice the shed.

Thus, for the Recorder, external time had stopped. Pretty soon he had lost the feeling of time passing. Once or twice a day he would walk out of his shed to look at the vehicles passing by, the pedestrians, and the sky above him. Of course, it's more likely he did not see anything but only pretended to be observing. There was no set time for his walking out of the shed—sometimes it was in the morning, sometimes in the afternoon, sometimes in the middle of the night. At the beginning he didn't know what he was doing himself. After several days it dawned on him that he was now classifying time according to his own subjective will. This was a brand-new kind of time. From then on he was going to live in this kind of time, and he had decided this himself.

Once upon a time there was such a Recorder. Yet this was not a very important thing because for us nothing that cannot be proved is important. We only recognize that there existed this person, we saw him and remembered him—we said so in 1990.

The inner world of the Recorder was more and more carefree. He could hear ten thousand horses galloping in his chest, and he felt the temperature of his blood rising and rising. Every thump of his heart would intoxicate him in the extreme. But he still could not see that miraculous image. Even if he had seen it, he could not have described it because he had abandoned his skill and he no longer knew how to describe. That was the source of his secret sorrow. Yet this sorrow itself was the spring of his happiness, and this could never be known by others.

As he walked out of his shed, he felt vaguely, his whole body and heart, that he was walking into that image. He could see nothing, but people saw him watching the passing cars. Thus the time that he calculated subjectively was increasing. He felt deeply that there would no longer be any recording. Yet in comparison to his former recording career, he felt that the present life was fixed, like an iron railroad that drove straight into the emptiness ahead. Although the forms in his imagination were still obscure, he was no longer bothered by this because he didn't need to express anything. He was only recording inside his own mind. This, of course, was only our guess because nobody knew.

The white-haired old woman had come several times. She stayed longer and longer in the shed. People saw her touching the Recorder's forehead with her ice-cold fingers, but that's all. Both sides had kept their silence. This was something that people noticed in passing but forgot about immediately afterward. Every time after the old woman left, the Recorder would go out of the shed at a quick pace. He would stand up straight on a rock placed by the roadside for road construction and focus his glances on the sky, searching anxiously for something. What was there in the sky? Of course, there was nothing. The Recorder would descend from the stone disheartened. He would ponder gloomily for a while, then become cheerful again.

On the street, cars streamed by; the battered shed, resembling a lonely island, shuddered endlessly.

ANONYMITIES

She never arrived when he expected. To put this another way, she always appeared in his apartment just at the moment he thought she would. Every time she arrived he saw in his mind's eye a clear image—a triangle with a grayish white fog along its edges. Now she had arrived once more. Sitting lightly on the table, she was jabbering something to him. When she sat down, the table did not move the least bit, though her glance was as blazing hot as it had been on other occasions, enough to make him feel a pressure he was very familiar with. She took his cup to get herself a drink of water. After she finished, she tilted the mug toward the sunlight and examined it for a long time. Then she waved it in the air as if she were ladling something. *"Gudong-gudong-gudong,"* she gurgled, and his Adam's apple bobbed twice accordingly. Usually every gesture of hers would lead directly to some physical response from him.

Perhaps because she had walked very fast when she came, he could smell the faint sweat on her body. This displeased him a little bit. Oddly, she had seemed never to perspire when she was young, and he had gotten used to her without perspiration. As soon as he sat down, he sank deep into memory. Yet this memory was constantly interrupted by the sound she was making. That sound came from her riffling through sheets of paper. She had picked up a stack of white paper from his drawer and was shuffling the leaves over and over as if she had found a way to entertain herself. Her pointed nails were pressing into those sheets, her shoulders were trembling, and her nostrils emitted a faint whistling full of satisfaction. So he stopped his reminiscing and stared at her playing her game as if he were somewhat fascinated.

The fact is he had never considered her age seriously. Somehow he felt he had known her for a relatively long time. Therefore, she could not be very young. But from the very beginning, he could not figure out her age. When he asked her, she replied that she didn't know, and she added that it was because there was no way she could know. As for him, at the time he was in his prime. Generally speaking, it had never occurred to him that another person's age could become a problem. However, the relationship between them grew in phases. Under careful analysis, it was very similar to the growth process of a plant from the time of its sprout breaking through the earth until the time of its withering away. But he could barely distinguish which period in their relationship corresponded to which stages of the plant's growth. He always felt that the whole matter was very vague and wouldn't be clarified until the last minute.

At present, her calmly turning over the pages gave him a feeling of perfect peace. In the distant past, she used to be impatient. Sometimes she could even be rude. He still remembered that she had thrown his favorite blue-flowered porcelain mug out the window. She had also thrown away some other things. That day, when outside the window the sky was filled with galloping clouds, the two of them had lain on the bed side by side for a long, long time. Their bodies had turned bloody red. Suddenly she had crawled over him and thrown out that porcelain mug. They both heard the cup shatter. After she had gone, he went downstairs looking for the broken mug. He saw that the thick grass in the garden had become blackish green and as tall as a human figure.

She had also criticized his residence. According to her description, he was jammed amongst crowded skyscrapers and everywhere surrounded by irritating noise. He was not very clear about his own environment. He was born in this apartment and had been living here ever since. There was a period when she sealed all the windows and doors with thick craft paper, turning the room into a dungeon filled with body odor. After doing this she disappeared for a fairly long time. When she arrived again, it appeared that she did not even notice that he had torn away all the craft paper. It was then that he knew she had a problem with forgetfulness.

The moment he thought of this, her hands stopped flipping the paper. With her shining glance she stared at his forehead. Stretching out her hand, she picked up the empty mug and made another gesture of ladling water.

"You are reminiscing about something." She said these words clearly. Then she jumped down from the table and walked toward the corner of the room. She stood there silently. He heard the clock at the station chime three P.M. Outside the window the air was a bright white.

"You have come and gone, gone and then come, numerous times. Now I don't even care whether you are coming or going. Sometimes I don't even know whether you are going or coming." This he said while facing the window. He didn't want her to hear too clearly. When he turned around she had disappeared, leaving her faint sweaty odor in the air.

That was the longest night. He paced up and down in the dimly lit morgue of the hospital, uncovering every corpse for identification, once, twice, three times, four times. . . . At four o'clock in the morning he returned to his apartment, cold sweat covering his body, feeling dizzy. She was already waiting in the shadow at the turn of the staircase.

She threw herself into his bosom, trembling. As soon as they entered the room, she closed all the curtains and refused to turn on the light. Her hair gave off the heavy odor of the morgue as well as the odor of the frosty wind of early morning. She made him smell those corpses again.

"There were altogether fifty-three," he whispered into her ear.

After she warmed up, she groaned faintly. Then she said confidently: "It's all in vain. You! Why didn't you recognize me? You searched again and again without ever finding me. I know in your mind there is another person, yet it's all in vain!"

That morning both of them were so ardent. In the dim light he noticed that her eyebrows had turned a deep red and her pointed nails were glittering.

"I have looked and looked, looked and looked, oh!" he

groaned falling into that bottomless cave, his whole body entangled by tentacles. His thumb had started bleeding. "Now my whole body is covered with that odor. I never expected to be like this. Maybe it has been this way from the very beginning. Is it true that my sense of smell is developing day by day?"

"Let's analyze it together," she said, flipping on the light. He dared not look at her in the dazzling light, so closing his eyes he turned around to face the wall.

"So you haven't recognized me even once?" Stroking his back tenderly she continued, "Do you feel that's difficult? It's not really! You know that there's a tiny mole under my left ear. Why did you forget to check their ears? Altogether there were only fifty-three people, yet you wasted a whole night. Ever since we parted last time I just knew you would go to a place like that. It can be said that you have been looking for that person ever since you were born. But you didn't know it when you were young. That's all. Next time make sure you don't forget to check those ears."

He woke up when the big clock at the station was striking nine. He could hear the rustling sound she was making in the room. Forcing his eyes open, he saw that she was pasting up the craft paper again. One of her long legs was planted on the table, the other on the windowsill. Her shoulders rose and fell. She was completely focused and meticulous. Without turning her head, she knew he had awakened. With one forceful jump, she sprang to the bed, then rolled over his body to the floor. She crawled to the door quietly, opened it, and disappeared into the darkness.

Waiting is unbearable, especially that kind of waiting for which there is no clear termination. In those protracted days he realized the full benefits of the craft paper. Sometimes he would not leave the apartment for a long time. In the darkness he completely forgot how many days had passed. In addition, once he closed the door and breathed only the air of the two of them, this made him calm down. With the craft paper on the window and the door, he imagined himself as a mole. Occasionally he would be lured by his fantasy, then he would open a tear in the craft paper to look at the bright whiteness outside the window. Every time he would be startled and his heart would thump.

He only went outside deep in the night when the station clock struck twelve and when there were scarcely any pedestrians on the street. As a result, it was almost natural that he should participate in the murder. This he did with a fruit knife in collaboration with a tall masked man. It was on the ground floor of his apartment building that this person struck an old man with a stick. As the victim was falling slowly, he dashed over and stabbed at the position of the old man's heart in his chest. He couldn't pull his knife out. With the knife in his chest, the old man mumbled something. Hurriedly, he turned back the old man's ear. Without a doubt, under his left ear there was a mole. From it spurted a drop of blood. The big masked man shouted, pushed him aside, lifted the corpse, and walked toward the riverbank at a quick pace, leaving him standing there alone in a daze.

"This is your first time to do such a thing," the masked

man sneered at his back. "You are looking for some kind of proof. Somebody told you a certain method, yet it cannot bear any result. I've seen this kind of thing often. Don't believe anybody's method. You'll get used to it if you do it more often."

The whole matter drove him to distraction for a long time.

Whenever he returned to his apartment early in the morning and passed that long, pitch-dark corridor, he would hold his breath to listen closely, hoping she would jump out from her hiding place, yet every time he was disappointed. She hadn't been to his apartment for three months. He knew she had very casual habits; therefore, this time maybe she had forgotten. He opened and closed the door, more and more carefully, attempting to keep her odor in the room for the longest time, although amidst that odor was the sweaty smell which had once aroused his unhappiness.

One night as soon as he lay down, someone knocked three times clearly on his windowpane. Jumping up he opened the window, yet there was only the wind blowing outside. He remembered that he was living on the tenth floor and a person couldn't possibly hang outside the window. At that instant there flashed in his mind's eye that triangle, now with red light along its edges. It was humming. Unexpectedly, she did not appear.

The last few days of waiting, he was full of hatred. He tore away all the craft paper, smashed the window glass, crumpled up the paper that bore her fingernail marks, and disassembled the bed in which he had slept with her. Then he left the apartment and wandered aimlessly along the river early in the morning.

All of a sudden he saw her standing in a boat filled with passengers, one long leg on top of the rail along the deck. Her torn clothing was streaming in the wind, and she was staring at the water. Afterward she saw him and smiled blankly. She pointed at her temple and then at the river. He didn't understand her meaning, and he became extraordinarily annoyed by this lack of understanding, but all he could do was wave madly and fruitlessly at her while running breathlessly along the riverbank adjacent to the boat. He must have appeared to be overrating his physical abilities ridiculously. The boat was pulling away gradually. She had left the deck for the cabin. The whistle blew twice wickedly.

He stopped. Was this boat going back to the city or leaving it? Clutching his head, he pondered and pondered. Finally he felt he should clarify the matter at the dock. He had been to the dock several times, yet at this instant he couldn't remember which direction he should go. Then he recalled that he had discussed this problem with her late at night. She had insisted that this was a permanently unsolvable puzzle. As she was saying that, she made a boat with her palms sailing back and forth in front of him and blowing the whistle with her mouth, a sound not unlike the two he had just heard. It seemed that he should not go to the dock but rather to any other place of his own choosing. Right. He should go to that park in which they had first met. It was by a fence on the lawn that he had discovered her sitting in the open air. At the moment he had been overjoyed by the discovery, but now when he thought about it he found there were some doubtful elements within the emotions of the time.

He walked all day except for stopping by the roadside to eat two pieces of bread and some ice cream. It was not until dusk fell that he entered the park. There were great changes in the park. He couldn't recognize that section of lawn. Perhaps there had never been a lawn. Nor flowerbeds and gardeners. Everywhere there were low wooden houses resembling each other with their doors shut tight and people rattling the same thing inside each house. Between houses there were only very narrow walkways. Without care one might brush against the dirty, damp brick walls. He wandered back and forth among the houses, hearing those monotonous rattling voices rising up into the silent night sky forming a gigantic wave of voices rumbling over him.

Finally one door opened and there appeared a dark shadow. Quickly, he walked over and recognized the figure as the man who patrolled the park. He appeared much older now. He asked the old man the direction of the original lawn and how he could exit from this group of houses.

"You can never find it, nor can you exit because it is night now." He guessed that the old man was laughing at him with a bit of contempt. "At night everything looks exactly the same, and you might feel that if you came more often. There haven't been any tourists for quite a few years because it's too monotonous. Perhaps you're the only tourist who's been here for many years. Yet that's no use. You can't stay on. I'm going in. I can't stay outside for too long." He closed the door sharply and snapped off the light inside. In one instant all the lights in all the wooden houses were turned off and the chattering stopped. It was dark all around except for the vague silhouettes of the houses. He felt his way along the brick walls. "It's too monotonous here. It's easy for your attention to drift. Please watch out," the old patrolman said, although where he was standing could not be made out. Yet his words were reassuring. Standing for a while gazing over those vague, dark mushrooms in front of him, he realized it was time for him to return to his apartment.

This time she was waiting for him at the front gate of his building. In the glow of dawn her smile was as fresh as a new leaf.

"I went to the place where we met for the first time. It's so strange that it turned out to be a stone pit, because what I remembered is so much richer," he said, feeling bubbles rise in his lungs. "I hadn't realized until now that this whole thing has had a decisive influence on me."

"No individual thing has decisive significance for you," she said.

The door had been blown open. Wind blew in through the broken window glass. She tittered. Picking up a fairly big piece of broken glass, she stared at it, facing the sunshine. The edge of the glass cut her finger. Blood dripped onto the other glass. The sun shone on them. They appeared gaily colored.

"It's not necessary to go to that park or stone pit often. We only met there incidentally. You only need to think of one place in your mind, and that place becomes your destiny." Putting her cut finger into her mouth, she sucked with force.

She said vaguely, "That's all it is." After she finished the sentence, she spat out a big mouthful of blood, making the whole room smell of blood. Her finger was still dripping. Suddenly she said, "I'm leaving." Turning around, she walked out. Like a gust of wind, she ran down the staircase, leaving a trail of blood in the corridor.

Returning to his apartment, he covered the window again with craft paper and assembled the bed that had been dismantled. Then he lay down deep in thought amidst the thick smell of blood.

He remembered the time when they had gotten to know each other. She had been full of vigor, indulging in fantasies. Every day she never tired of looking for something new. Once they had even climbed to the top of the commercial building in the city and thrown a bag of garbage onto the crowds below. When they descended the building she was giggling endlessly. Now when he reminisced about it, the memory seemed unimportant. But at the time he had been full of joy. Often there had been partings, but every time he had been full of hope and imagination, not the impatience and hatred that now possessed him. Since when had she turned so gloomy and rigid toward him, become so indifferent toward the things he cared for? Once he had thought her to be a warmhearted woman. At the beginning he thought she was just worn out and would not come again. Yet after a while she had come back. Maybe the time between two visits grew a little bit longer, but she had never left without looking back. This morning was the first time in a long time that he had seen her laugh. He had doubted if she could even smile.

Before he fell into sleep he struggled to the window and looked down by raising the craft paper. He saw her standing on the street in front of the grocery store raising her injured hand. She also saw him, so using the other hand she pointed at her feet and nodded her head. He didn't understand the meaning of her gesture, not even once. Whenever he thought of that he felt very disheartened. He fell into sleep dejected and slept very deeply.

When he awoke he noticed many bloody finger marks on the wall put there by her the day before. At the time, he hadn't noticed, but after one day the blood marks had turned a bit black. They looked like leeches crawling on the wall, making him uneasy. Watching those leeches—her masterpiece—he remembered she had always been against him, and she was always mysterious in her ways. Nobody could predict what she was going to do in the next minute. With her back toward him and her face toward the wall, she said in a harsh voice, "People like me had better hide themselves in order not to upset people." He turned her face back and saw an expression similar to that of a little deer being chased. He was so touched that he almost cried out. That time they stayed together for three days without leaving each other for one minute. At dusk, they would open the window and watch the sunset. Standing at the window hugging tightly against each other, they exchanged breath. She even leapt into the air naughtily. Every time she did so, he would be so frightened that his face turned pale and he would pull her down tightly. In the short three days, she forgot about things like the craft paper. She was jumping up and down and saying crazy things. Perhaps it was because both of them were young at the time, and also they were confused by the emotion caused by pity. That was the longest time she stayed. It was so long that he even had some illusion that she would stay forever. But, of course, this result was not to be.

Later on they could no longer share such intimate talk. Instead, they would talk vaguely and exchange evasive glances. When they met on the street, they would greet each other with some obscure gesture the same way she did in front of the grocery store. This method was decided on by her, and he went along with it. It appeared that they had a tacit understanding, but in reality they were very distant. Even at the climax of making love, the feeling was vague and ambiguous as if they were thousands of mountains and thousands of rivers apart. It was totally different from lovemaking with other women when he was young. Every time when it was finished he would be overwhelmed by an infinite confusion, his head feeling as if a bird's nest had grown there. At those moments he meant to dash out and chase her, yet he had no confidence whatsoever. Finally he would drop the idea. It was not because of his self-esteem, but just because he felt it would be in vain.

As she got older, her tone and glances became colder, and their distance and grievances grew deeper until they began holding grudges against each other. Once she revealed to him that their present situation was the best, exactly what she wanted, because it reflected the truth of their relationship. If they were, instead, to do nothing but stand at the window enjoying the setting sun, she would have to jump down and never return. However, such a relationship was horrifying to him. He couldn't remember how many times he had sneaked into the morgues of those hospitals to check the corpses, feeling exhausted from anxiety and fear. And he never dared to doze off in the morgues because there was always a red-eyed cat glaring at him fiercely. The days of waiting were endless spiritual torture because there were no lines or color there, just complete emptiness. It was during that period that his mouthful of strong teeth started to loosen.

Then an odd thing happened—she bit a small piece of flesh from his arm. According to her, she did it unintentionally, and she promised that nothing similar would happen in the future. The wound was not deep and healed quickly, leaving only a tiny scar. But whenever he thought of it he shivered with fear. When he inquired as to where the flesh that she bit off went, she replied that she had swallowed it. When she said that, she appeared furious, sending a chill up his spine. Yet he missed her every minute, every second, even missed the long bench by the fence on the lawn. It was there that she sat in the open air and gave him that magnificent talk. Besides there was that warm, sliding sun, the rising warmth from the earth, making him mistake her for a fine young maiden. She had forgotten all that long ago. Whenever he raised the issue later on, she appeared bored. Using her strong index finger, she would make a decisive gesture to stop his story. "I was only waiting for a boat there," she would say shortly and drily. He couldn't help feeling very indignant.

It was fairly recently that she had gone to extremes in her appearance. In the past, she had never paid much attention to her appearance. Yet she always dressed simply and comfortably. Her clean underwear gave off a fine fragrance. But recently she had put on a set of extremely ugly men's clothes and refused to change. They had become dirtier and dirtier, shabbier and shabbier. She even boasted about them, saying they were so convenient. In the past, time spent washing clothes was nothing but trouble for her, and so on. Then she would say that since she could no longer smell the odor of the dirty clothes, why should she spend time pursuing formalities? It was even acceptable that she would not take a bath from now on. The only reason she kept taking baths and washing her hair was as a compromise with his strange habits, despite the fact that she felt they were vulgar. This took place in the third month after she cut her finger. They saw each other at the dock. Both appeared a little bit wan and sallow, a little bit melancholy. He told her he had heard someone knocking at the window of his apartment late at night. Could it have been her?

"That's impossible. When I'm outside I never think of you. You've known for a long time that I don't have a memory." She wrinkled her nose slightly. "Can you guess if I have just returned or am planning to leave? An eternal puzzle." She pointed at the passing boats and asked him to look. The river appeared vast and endless with boats floating as if in outer space.

He did not answer her question because he knew it had no answer. It was she who had told him that. Lowering his head, he saw that her bare feet wearing the sandals had turned a bit rough.

"Shall we return to the apartment?" he asked.

"No," she said harshly. "From now on let's see each other here. It's very convenient for both of us. Of course, there's no way for me to arrange the date ahead of time. You'll just have to come often and see if I'm here. That shouldn't be too difficult." Arrogantly she threw back her short hair, putting her hands into her wide pockets.

"I turned over a person's ear, and I saw that mole," he said. "At the moment I was in a unique situation."

"There are such cheap marks everywhere," she sneered in contempt. "Now you'd better go. Let me see you disappear among the crowd."

"It's you who has raised the issue."

"It's possible that I have said so. Don't always remember. You should forget along the way. Why don't you go?"

At that moment a gray boat was anchoring. She raised her long legs and boarded the ship. This time she did not look back. The boat gradually sailed away as if it were departing into the vast universe.

But he knew there was a thread linking him with that boat. He turned around and walked away. At every step he felt his chest being pulled at painfully by that thread. At the same time, that triangle in his mind's eye was shooting out gold sparks.

APPLE TREE
IN THE CORRIDOR

The Little Gold Ox

There's frost outside. One sniff of the glistening air tells me that. Frosty mornings always create discord among people. I inhale deeply and smile quietly. Then I chuckle unexpectedly, giving out the queer "heh-heh" that I often find myself producing lately. The frigid, discordant wind rattles the window frame repeatedly. In the clear sky floats a ball of red silk thread, spinning and bobbing, up and down, circling around. I can't get the window open. I know that the bright sunlight is only a deception—the bitter cold would freeze my nose. "I have a very sensitive nose," I say to myself, nodding firmly and staring out at the frozen earth.

Everything gives the appearance of being real. The little gold ox on the tea table is moving again, its tail swinging. "You, old boy, are already fifty-seven this year," the mask on the wall says to me. The mask is covered with a fuzz of white mold resembling a beard. It reminds me of a jade green cobblestone that I saw embedded between tree roots poking up out of the soil at the side of the highway. One dusk I attempted to dig it out with a small knife.

On that last day, a huge crowd swarmed into the city's streets. With surprise I discovered the scene from a very high vantage point just as it was happening. Of course, these people have long ago disappeared completely, and the incident has left me with no solid impression. At the beginning, I had pried open a window to climb into the building. In every empty room I found a pale mask. On the wall the swinging shadows of the wild vines made threatening gestures, reminding me of haunted houses. Then my face went moldy. Every time I look into the mirror, I see a hazy white oval. This is so disgusting.

My father's brown leather jacket, ornamented with multicolored birds' feathers, still hangs in his closet. As soon as the closet is opened, the feathers stand up, as if they were about to fly away. He spent his whole life traveling in the mountains. He looked forever travel-stained and smelled of grass. Leaning over a greasy table at a bar, he once discussed with me an intestinal disease and its cure. He was laden with anxieties.

"Before dawn, the Seven-Li Fragrance always causes me migraine, and it smells of seawater, too. The Seven-Li Fragrance must be blossoming on both sides of a seaside highway. I can imagine the place." After these words, he lowered his head and fell into sleep.

He died of an intussusception. It wasn't until three days later that we, together with a doctor, found him under a Chinese chestnut tree. His travel bag was stuffed with stinking orioles and turtledoves killed with an airgun days before. We simply left him there. Out of fear, we pretended to have forgotten about burying him. On our way back, Mother and I kept talking loudly to control our fright. The doctor was walking in front of us. His white coverall was stained with bird droppings, large smears of yellowish green. Every now and then, Mother cast sharp sidelong glances at me with her aged eyes. I knew that she had guessed my thought. So I jabbered on at random, ill at ease. I mentioned a past incident in a watermelon field, and asked if she could remember which day it was.

"That's very odd." She halted and said hesitantly, "How could I have given birth to you? I have so much doubt about it. Just at that moment, I lost my memory. So the thing cannot be confirmed."

I carry on my father's dream. Time and again, I feel so vividly that I touch the paving of the highway warmed by the sun, and hear mimicking cock crows. This also happens at the instant just before dawn when I smell the Seven-Li Fragrance. The dreams are drawn out, with an extremely long white thread fluttering behind each one of them just like a kite. But what is the matter with the ostrich? Ever since my father's death, my intestines have started to twist and turn. Glaring at me, Mother ordered simply, "You have to go to the mountains." Then she threw the blood-stained travel bag at my feet.

I intend to look for a kind of herb that can cure intestinal diseases.

Upstairs there used to live a fellow with sunglasses. This guy was about fifty, though he told everybody that he was twenty-seven. One day he entered our kitchen. With one leap, he jumped into the cistern and refused to come out. He lived in the cistern for several years like a hippo, splattering water all over the kitchen. Every time I stepped into the kitchen, he would let loose a torrent of abuse. He then disappeared with my third sister. One day when the sweet scent of the Seven-Li Fragrance was spreading unchecked, we met on a cliff. My third sister exposed my little trick with a single remark. I seemed to hear them whistling to pigeons in the bamboo forest, but I dared not turn my head, because the turkey behind the rock made me very nervous. Venus rattled past my ear, and a surreal rosy color appeared along the rim of the sky. After that they disappeared together. How very suspicious.

However, a frosty morning still makes me ready to do something—it's my nature. So I put on my cap and shoulder the traveling bag. I purse my wrinkled mouth to whistle, and kick out my legs, causing a messy fit of noise in my intestines—gestures preliminary to a long journey. In the mirror, I see the mask spit and say, "Fifty-seven." Then I take off my cap and sniff the greasy brim, recalling the secret of my father's artificial leg. He kept this secret from me very carefully. His leg was of high quality and showed almost no marks of being unreal. In fact, I did not know about it until after his death. For several days, Mother appeared to be on tenterhooks. Finally, she couldn't control her urge to tell me that the reason she did not bury my father was because of the artificial leg. She never failed to have an attack of epilepsy every time she saw that smooth pink object.

"His own leg was okay, but he broke it intentionally in order to fix that wretched thing on—one of his wild fantasies. Wearing that stupid thing, he declared forever to people that he had become a young bachelor again. He even boasted to me that the artificial leg was as soft and light as cotton, and claimed his nerves had grown into the leg. He tried to create a special image of himself."

I found the herb in the house of my third sister's classmate. It was planted in a huge pot placed on the windowsill facing south. It dawned on me that this woman was also once tortured by intestinal diseases. Her room was littered with old newspapers, revealing her unbearable affliction.

Everything that happened in the past is real. At the time when I met my third sister on the cliff, pigeons were whispering in the woods, and it seemed to be drizzling. I had extreme trouble opening my tired eyelids. Then all of a sudden, she started talking from behind me, laying bare my trick.

The little gold ox is pacing back and forth on the tea table. A lump of frozen cloud drifts by the window. A dolphin is trapped between the dead branches of a camphor tree. Numerous roosters are crowing one after another. The mask on the wall is talking again: "Fifty-seven years old." This mask used to be an old fellow picking odds and ends from the garbage. Purposefully, he hanged himself from our doorframe, naked.

1. OUR FAMILY SECRETS

"What are the long-legged mosquitoes humming about? It's so ridiculous." Mother's voice came unexpectedly from the shadow behind the bed. She had been hiding in that corner since the last rain. She wanted people to think she had disappeared. Excitedly, she found a big umbrella and covered herself completely with it. "My body is puffed up like an oxygen pillow." In the drawer she had found a five-headed needle, and she was punching it into her skin. With her teeth clenched, she punched and pressed, saying, "I've got to get rid of some water, or I'll be dead."

I wanted to tell her something about the summer. Hesitantly, I opened my mouth: "The hornet's nest was humming on the bare branch. Something was swinging in the air . . . Once I lost a wallet. Obviously you remember the incident. It was stolen by a guy with a beard. The streets at the time were covered by white bed sheets, which shone in the sun. Children were running around carrying torches. Don't you feel that the needles are pushing against rotten meat?"

All my family members had undivulged secrets. They must have seemed like frightening people. My father, for instance, was a very unusual person. I never understood him. To me, he was analogous to insects, because he always gave me a feeling of beetle shells. He would sneak in every night after supper had already started. Darting to the table, he would fill his bowl with rice while scanning the other dishes. He chewed and swallowed all the good dishes before banging his bowl down on the table and fleeing.

"Father is suffering some internal agony," my third sister would say, showing the whites of her eyes. Her voice resembled a noodle hanging in the damp air. She always gnawed at the rims of the bowls at mealtime. As a result, all of our blue china bowls had chipped edges. I saw with my own eyes that she swallowed the chips with her rice. For a cure to her asthma, she had, up to that time, eaten more than a thousand earthworms. Actually, she drank them after melting them down in sugar. "Isn't that miraculous!" Panting, she would put on an expression of wonder.

"Your third sister, it's hard to say," Mother commented in a sarcastic tone. "Did you hear her thumping the bed? The doctors think she's having endocrinopathy. It's a subtle ailment."

I was about to reply when I heard a deafening noise from the upstairs neighbor. According to my reconnoitering, the guy had been fooling around with an iron drilling rod. The cement floor of his apartment was covered with small holes like a honeycomb. Mother continued indifferently, turning a deaf ear to the noise from upstairs: "I can see through anybody's tricks. I have become so ingeniously skillful that I am close to being a master of magic. Day after day, I sit in this corner, puncturing myself with needles in my fight against the fluids. Sometimes I simply forget you are my children. Whenever I recall the past, the wild mountains and deserted forests appear in my mind's eye, stars fall down like fireworks, and the black figure of your father hangs from a branch of the tree. Quickly he has turned into what he is now. It's just too fast."

At the window pane appeared a pair of huge sunglasses. That was the guy from upstairs coming down to spy on our reaction to his dirty trick. He never forgot to put on his sunglasses, believing that no one could recognize him this way.

"This guy is suffering from ringworm on his feet." Mother turned her small, flat head distractedly. Every time the back of her head brushed her shoulders, wisps of dry, broken hair drifted into the air. "Can't you smell the liquid for ringworms? Nearly everyone has some subtle ailment. But everyone racks his brain for ways to appear to be healthy."

Sunglasses entered the room. Dressed in a white coverall and with a stethoscope hanging at his chest, he appeared full of dignity and dash. To show off, he raised the stethoscope solemnly to listen to the wall for a long time. Then, in an air of pretended wisdom, he said in a lowered voice: "I am a medical doctor. I live at No. 65 on Thirteenth Avenue. Your family has some serious problems."

"Medical doctor? Perfect, doctor!" Mother shrilled from the shadow. "I'd like you to have a look at my ears! My ears are so sensitive. Is there any way to cure them, like giving them anesthesia?"

He bounced up and down several times on the spot, before disappearing completely.

"This is called the invisible method," Mother told me quietly.

"A horse in heat, a tragic reality?" My third sister drifted into the room. Softly, she descended on the bedside. Supporting her chin with her fine, vinelike fingers, she was spellbound, staring into the air. "Such people have a special kind of organ," she added, her eyes filled with rheumy tears. "All disasters are caused by this unlucky smell!" She dashed into her bedroom and started sobbing heavily. In fact, she would have felt much better if she had set herself down to crochet lace. When she was young, she used to sit quietly by the window, crocheting her lace. A slight touch by others would cause her nose to bleed. I was quite surprised to see her becoming so forward.

After dark every day, I started looking for my family members. From this room to that, I found that they had all disappeared totally. The wind swayed the little electric bulb, making the light turn bloody red all of a sudden. The west wind was blowing hard. I was feeling uneasy at not being able to figure out where they were hiding.

Then I formulated a plan. After supper one day, I asked Mother to lend me her needles. "What for?" Her eyes looked like billiard balls ready to roll.

"You always abandon me, thinking that I am useless. But on the contrary, I have my own skill. It may well be that I am more nimble than you are." While talking I grabbed her sleeve tightly, fearing that she might suddenly disappear.

"I'm-sleeping-in-the-trunk," she said, enunciating word by word and glaring at me. "Every night you pace around in my room, as anxious as an ant in a hot pot. Once you even stepped on my eyeball. Didn't you feel it? I just can't sleep. See the two huge dark rings under my eyes? They're caused by in-somnia."

At night, I did notice there was a worn-out trunk, on which hung a rusty bronze lock. So I entered her room to look for the trunk, but there was nothing in the corner.

"You're wasting your energy," she chuckled drily. "Very often you remember something, but you won't know that there is no such thing until you try to look for it. Once upon a time, there was some dough in our cupboard, and it was all moldy. Last year, I was digging in the cupboard in our attic, looking for that dough. I had been searching for a year when finally the stairs collapsed and I fell. Your third sister told me that the cupboard was not the original one, I had remembered wrong. Your third sister has her mind stuffed with fantasies about men. I know that's the source of her disease. There's no hope for a cure." She shrugged in resignation. "How do you feel about our apartment?" Her triangular eyes gazed at me with interest.

"I've been searching for you. My legs are so sore that I can no longer raise them. I pitch stones on the ground. You must have heard it, haven't you?"

"What trunk are you talking about? It's just a story that I told you before. I warned you that it's a waste of energy. It's so stupid of you to search everywhere. You also mentioned three-needle acupuncture. You sound like a snake player. Are you really so afraid? Wait till you reach my age, then you won't be afraid anymore. In your arrogant memory there must be many types of broken trunks. They are hidden here and there. You believe they contain something. It's a phenomenon of youth, in fact . . ." She stopped short, impatiently examining the window behind me.

During the day I kept telling myself that I shouldn't forget to pay attention to those trunks at night. I wondered why I always forgot, and thought I should make a mark at those spots. Yet as soon as night arrived, my memory was befuddled. I turned this way and that, passing a trunk, a broom, a wallet, etc. But I just couldn't remember anything. Where were my family members? They should at least have left some clue.

Rats started a fight in the light fixture. The rats in this house were as big as cats. I covered the bulb with my pale hands to avoid attracting moths. The light was cold, and its rays penetrated to the depths of my heart. On the wall, I saw a projection of my heart. I intended to tell Mother about the summer. Suddenly all the kidney beans she had salted melted into stinking water and the Boston ivy drooped over. In the shadow, the bronze kettle rattled angrily. A cat climbed over the wall, at the foot of which there grew some castor oil plants. My third sister came by whistling. She had two bamboo leaves stuck in her nostrils. They had red spots on them and resembled dominoes.

There was nobody in Father's room, either. The air smelled of sweat. There was a banana peel on the stool. During the day he told me in secret that he had recently been engaged in catching locusts. With his own eyes he saw mother kill five flowery moths and dump them into the dried-up well at the back of the house. "Tomorrow I will climb the green mountain," he said, twisting his hips, and tapping the earthenware pot that he held against his chest like a little kid. "The locusts are flourishing there." He was enjoying the verb he used, his face glowing with health.

"I'd like to tell Mother something," I said.

"Your mother," he rolled his huge eyeballs with difficulty, trying to recall something. "She is not a reliable thing. Don't trust such a thing easily." He jumped high on one foot, spilling all of the sand out of the pot. "I've been sleeping in the cotton fiber. It's so quiet there, and no rats, either. How long have you been suffering from sleepwalking? It's certainly a painful ailment. I once had it, too. Now about Sunglasses, you don't need to guard against him, but treat him nicely. That guy is my friend. When dawn comes, we wander around, and at night, we sleep in the cotton fiber. One day when the Chinese scholar tree blossomed all in white, I squatted down at the corner of the street. Taking off my vest, I scratched myself as much as I could—I hadn't had a bath for the whole winter. Later on, I noticed somebody else squatting there. That was him, he was scratching also. Together we listened to the humming of the mosquitoes, and our bodies felt all warmed up."

The door banged open. "I just can't wash my hair." My third sister stood between father and me, with her hands on her hips and her hair let down. "Every time I wash my hair, my head gets light and drifty, like a balloon, and floats away from my neck. You simply cannot experience such a thing, no way! I'm just wasting my time." She sat heavily on the bedside, a hook from her bra strap unfastened. "Who understands my sorrow? In the blue sky, there flies a yellow weasel! Ah? Ah? . . ." She sang and panted in an odd tone and spat on the floor.

"She has an enlarged cervical vertebra." Father's nose wrinkled up. He threw something at the foot of the bed.

"Father?"

"Your mother will come and eat it. Do you know why your mother hides herself? She's trying to avoid rats. Last time I threw down a piece of cooked meat with maggots in it, but she ate it happily. Her stomach is rumbling with hunger. She eats everything I throw down. You may try, too!" Tightening his pants, he let out the aged, shrunken, smooth left leg. Then he threw his canvas bag onto his shoulder. With high spirits, he said, "I'm going to the green mountains today!"

I could hear him whistling outside the window.

Finally, I told Mother the story about the summer. I repeated it again and again, my face turning purple. Mother appeared half listening, smiling indulgently. With a bare foot she scratched her tightened calf muscle.

"That's right, when the sun rises, I will turn into a fat hen." In that instant, her pupils seemed to be melting. "The whole day, I squat in the woodpile under the eaves. Little children come and throw cobblestones at me. Eventually, one of them will break my spine." She suddenly stood up, her eyes turned left and right in an equivocal way. "Now I need to change my approach completely. I have displayed fortitude and resolution. Just now I have broken a window. You all believe that I've been kept in the dark, don't you? You, every one of you, what are you crying for underneath your quilts? Every day, just look at your swollen eyelids. I'm also making my own plans. You can't see through me, but you think you can do everything your own way now! That's why you're jabbering such nonsense to me."

Since a certain day, Mother had started to frighten us. She hid herself on purpose, yet she was present everywhere—underneath the bed, on top of the cupboard, behind the kitchen door, inside the cistern. Her deformed shadow drifted all over the place. The shadow was fat, swollen, purple in color, and smelled moldy. As a result, we walked quietly and spoke in whispers. Often when I was talking in Father's ear, she screamed, as if she were about to jump out. It scared the wits out of us. Yet when we looked around, she was nowhere to be found. And the scream was from the radio. At other times, she giggled in the shadow instead of screaming. The sound raised goose bumps on our bodies. My third sister was the first to burn out. Struggling out of her fits of hysteria, she searched for our missing mother, with a spade on her shoulder. At those moments, her face was purple, her neck stiff; she looked valiant and spirited. The base of the walls inside the house, the stove, and everything else had all been dug into a mess.

The day I suddenly realized that Mother had disappeared from this house forever, father was putting on his leg wrappings. "I'm going to the green mountains to fish for two months," he told me in high spirits. His cheeks were flushed with excitement.

"What shall we do about Mother?" I asked abruptly.

"I've raised a poisonous snake in the bushes. It comes out whenever I call it. Are you interested? We can catch locusts together."

"There's a poisonous snake I raised right under my bed." Mother's sharp voice resounded in the shadows.

Taking up his canvas bag, Father dashed out of the house like a young boy, his bag flopping against his skinny hips. "Two months!" he shouted back to me, raising two fingers, while running away.

I heard a suspicious sound behind me. When I turned around, I saw my third sister smashing her spade down on the dark spot where Mother's voice could be heard. A string of yellow sparks leapt from the cement.

"The buttons on that thing must be almost all gone, am I right?" I suddenly remembered.

My third sister never took me seriously. Dripping with black sweat, she was digging enthusiastically at the cement, her nostrils flared. "I've been sleeping too long. So I need to stretch my body a little," she defended herself. "You've been imagining that the house is collapsing. It's so vague. Why can't you think of something else? I can't understand how you've become such a misanthrope. Such people make me sick, sick." At noon, she had her nap half naked. She lay on her bed convulsing, stinking saliva dripping from her mouth. She usually slept like this until dusk and refused to have supper. When Father was home, he would peep into her open door, poke out his tongue and say, "What a miracle and wonder inheritance can play! Following the rule, what kind of decisive turning point will occur?" After such a remark, he felt he had somehow qualified himself to grab all the food in the house and take it away in his travel bag.

One rainy day, a soaking wet man staggered in. Wiping rainwater from his face, he bawled down to mother's shadow in the corner, addressing her in a shrill voice: "Hi, Mom!" Like a gust of wind, my third sister dashed over and wrapped him in a huge bath towel that had black spots on it. She rubbed and rubbed until his lips turned red and his eyeballs bloodstained. Then she fell to the floor and cried out, "It's awful to have a fiancé!" Then she suddenly became so muscular that she could carry the whole bundle wrapped inside the towel all the way to the bed. Carefully she put the bundle down, covered it with a quilt, and patted him to sleep.

"It's so uncomfortable to have a doctor at home." Mother's head stretched out like that of a snake.

"Who's that?"

"Sunglasses, of course. I knew long ago that Sunglasses was her fiancé. Now her illness will be healed. Such an awkward illness. Such things are totally strange." She drifted back beneath the bed.

"How could it be that the fence turns green? I've lost my stethoscope." The fiancé was groaning inside the bath towel. "The room is high in temperature. That's good. I feel sleepy when it's hot."

After the heavy rain, our house was full of spiderwebs. The slightest move would cause them to billow into one's eyes. My third sister was jumping about chasing spiders. Torn webs wafted all over the place.

"Oh, her youthful vitality." The fiancé opened one eye to enjoy the scene. "In my place, I have all sorts of insects. In the full of night, when I was wandering around outside, one of the insects must have sneaked into my bedding. This has occupied my mind, and I cry my heart out for that."

"But why did you make such a startling noise above us?" I asked him curiously. "Because of some inner fear?"

He hesitated. "The illness of your third sister bothers me day and night. It must be a very complicated syndrome."

All of a sudden, I had a desire to chat with him. Tugging his ear, I told him: "Every night this apartment turns empty. Everybody hides. Even the doors and windows disappear. It simply turns into a sealed iron box. I wander about, bumping into all kinds of things. In anxiety, I kick the wall till my toenails swell up. My third sister, she must have hinted to you. She believes that I never get up at night. She points out that it is my scattered quilt that proves this. It seems you are not hearing me. Tell me, is there any sound from my mouth?"

"The room is awfully hot." He was squint-eyed, his head hanging down, and he started to snore.

"You always tangle up everyone you meet like a beggar." My third sister slapped my hand and blew on the reddened ear of her fiancé. She gave me an angry stare, while rubbing his hair, and then yelled, "Scram!"

For the next several days, she and her fiancé occupied the whole house. Early every morning, they drove me out. Closing the door behind me, they simply turned the house into a lunatic asylum. A broom came flying out of the window facing the street, then a bag of plum cores. Once the thing flying out was Sunglasses himself. He was all black and blue and cried, "Acute changes are going on in your sister's body. Where did she get all that strength? Endocrinopathy is not a curable disease. The first time I saw her, she had bamboo leaves in her nostrils. That peddler selling popsicles yelled and yelled. It was so disgusting. My back was soaked with sweat, and my silk socks smelled . . ."

"It was summer," I reminded him.

"True. It was summer. My affliction of foul-smelling feet was cured. Your third sister ordered me to wash with soda water every day. But now I feel nothing is meaningful." Finally he observed me carefully. "Why can't a serious person like you involve yourself in some business, such as collecting snakeskins? Every time you approach me, I feel uncertain about you. Your existence is a problem. It seems that you've made up your mind that you are stuck here, and you never think of getting into something positive, for instance, snakeskins. You are just too much at ease. After all, this is a disease of the reproductive system. Your family . . ."

Once I saw my father while I was wandering around. He dashed out from behind a big tree and ran across the street. He tossed his canvas bag into the air, scattering little fish and tiny shrimp all over the ground. With just one flash of his army-green leg wrapping, he disappeared completely. I ran over and picked up the fish and shrimp, but then I realized that the little creatures in my hands were actually green worms and ants.

"Have you discovered that Father is completely done?" My third sister bent her two short legs and leaned on a lamppost. She continued: "He pretends that nothing has happened. Wandering around the street, he appears talented and unconventional, but it's a false image. I've experienced the disease of blockage in the urethra, so I know he is in great pain. We shake with laughter when we see him chatting with you in dead earnest about something like the green mountains. Every time he leaves the house, he sleeps in that run-down temple. There's some straw in the corner, and other people also sleep there. In fact, at the moment when I first communicated my love to the doctor, he was staying there, too. Once when I went there, Father jabbered to me all day about a dogskin vest. Over and over he explained that the vest had fallen beneath the floor of our original house. It fell through a hole in the floor. He also said some kind of dog-shit mold grew there as big as a fist. The reason he was wandering about was to look for that vest. That green mountain, I can see, is only a symptom of urethra blockage."

I walked into the collapsing temple, and saw several feral cats scurry away. Two black faces emerging from the straw pile told me that Father was no longer here. I understood that he had become too ashamed when he realized that I'd seen through his lies. I left the place in a hurry so he wouldn't feel too embarrassed. Turning my head, to my surprise, I found him making faces at me through the window. "I've been in the green mountains all the time!" He pointed two fingers at me. I was at such a loss that I felt deeply disheartened.

"You traitor!" My third sister dashed over from across the street and blocked my way. "Why did you go to that old temple? Ah? Who gave you the right to act on your own? You've degraded all of us! Now that old guy is chuckling behind the window. He thought that we instructed you to go there, you fool. So now we have all become the laughingstock of others!" She punched me angrily, and all the seams on her blouse burst open.

I'd hidden a hammer at the corner of the house. When all were in their hiding places and everything had quieted down, I felt my way to the window by the dim light from the street. Opening the window, I spat ferociously into the darkness. I saw my sputum flash in a ray of light, until my mouth became numb. My hammer clanged against the brick wall and made a dull, muffled echo. A light from some house flashed once. Who couldn't hear such deafening noise? Or could it be that my hand could never produce real sound? I hammered the whole night through, but in vain. In the morning I hid the hammer away in shame. My body ached all over. My third sister walked out of her bedroom, yawning. Her mouth smelled. She glared at me sneeringly, shrugged, and spat on the floor.

"Where has Mother gone?" I asked her with a straight face, wondering where she had emerged from.

My third sister jumped up with a scream in the middle of the room: "Stop your dirty tricks! You're an odd one to put on the face of savior. It's disgusting! You're the one who's sick! And you mistake me as the one! Who's not clear about such things? In this corridor of ours, this disastrous passage, such soul-stirring changes are taking place, don't you feel it? We'd be overjoyed if you left us! Yet you never leave; you're stuck here . . ."

It was obvious that Mother had disappeared. Why should they remain so straight-faced and deny it? A living being should be seen and touched, yet mother could be neither of these. But whenever I raised the issue, they blew up. Their temper was definitely getting worse.

When I stepped into the kitchen, a large black figure emerged from the cistern. The soaking creature howled at me, "Look out!" It turned out to be the fiancé. How could he hide in the cistern? And what a coincidence that he rose up to threaten me just at the moment when I entered the kitchen. There must have been some ulterior motive there. "I'm a doctor." Dripping wet, he stood erect and continued. At the same time, he kept poking my cheeks with his wet finger: "Your whole family has that complicated syndrome. Without my care, God knows what misery you would be living in. People in dire straits all want to save face, and they pretend that nothing has happened. When I was living above you, I could hear your third sister hit her head against the bed frame in pain. The reason I stamped on the floor so hard was to reduce her pain, in fear that she might run upstairs and have a fit. You're the sickest of all your family. I've been watching your behavior all the time. I had been hidden in the water for more than two hours when you entered the kitchen. I'm shivering with cold." His eyes grew dim, and he started sneezing, one after another, until my third sister rushed in and carried him off like a gust of wind blowing away a fallen leaf.

Father had been spreading the rumor that he left home because of unbearable oppression. He also said he had been living on fish and shrimp, but it wasn't true, because he sneaked back home to steal food. It wasn't even discreet stealing but brazen robbery. Though at every theft, they all pretended not to notice. They played their roles so well that I was tempted to think they had trouble with their eyesight. Maybe they were able not to see something—for instance, father pilfering food—if they didn't want to see it. On the other hand, they could always see something, for instance, our disappeared mother, if they wanted to see it. Therefore, they discriminated against people with eyes like mine. Sunglasses once commented about me, "It's horrifying for a person to develop such an unfortunate temperament as his."

For several days, I'd felt terribly dizzy. I dared not look at people, or even look out the window. Wrapping my head in a cotton-padded quilt, I had lain in bed for three days and three nights. The fourth day, I supported myself by leaning against the wall and moved to the door muddleheadedly. I stood there clutching the doorframe. In the wind, everything was tilted and had several silhouettes. It was impossible to see anything clearly. Under that dead tree sat my mother. She had her nylons peeled down and was scratching her swollen feet. Because of the wind, her white hair stood toward the sky. She looked like a primitive figure. "Mo-ma!" I called out in a funny way. She turned her head toward me. I saw an unfamiliar, vague face. This was a young woman. "Your illness is serious. You've had that disease for a long time. It started from inside, and the hope for recovery is slim. You should keep this fact covered up." She made a resolute gesture with a sneer.

My mouth felt very heavy, and the wind was so noisy I couldn't hear my own voice. So I shouted, "I can't see anything clearly! My head has a bellowing inside! You are young, so why is your hair all white?"

"That's the problem with your eyes," she sneered viciously. "From now on, just don't use your eyes anymore. It's much better that way. Your dizziness is caused solely by the eyes. I have a relative who is suffering from the same disease. He used his eyes so much that eventually his eyeballs fell out. Since you can't see things anymore, you have to admit it as a defect. Ambition will lead to no good ending."

I remembered that red snake berries once grew along the wall. Bending low and closing my eyes, I could feel them with my trembling fingers.

The sky was dim; everything underneath it looked like some kind of fluid. Three white geese flew through the mist like swimmers, then in one white flash they all disappeared.

My finger touched a snail. My heart quivered, and my body was covered with goose bumps. Forcing my eyes open, I saw the woman fall back, farther and farther away. My eyeballs expanded so fast that I felt they might drop out of their sockets.

"I've also been sick," she waved her hand at last. "You've seen that my feet are swollen like carrots. I feel terrible every time I touch them . . . I've been taking extra precautions to hide it."

"You, go lie down." My third sister jabbed my back and said with boredom, "Your spine is like a snake in puberty."

Half conscious, I felt my way back to bed and covered myself with the quilt. Even inside the quilt, I could still hear the noise of my sister rummaging through chests and cupboards and also the howling and crying of her fiancé being chased and beaten. My third sister was getting more and more unbridled daily. She let down her hair and wore shorts and T-shirts. She beat my quilt with a broom. I had never thought she possessed such strength. In fact, her asthma was only one of her little dramas made up out of nowhere. She always succeeded at whatever she involved herself in. I curled up inside the quilt, soaking with sweat, waiting for the fit to die down.

It was getting dark, and I still couldn't get up. I dug out a broken mirror and looked into it. I saw a vague lump of a face, with two reddened balls rolling around in it. They must have been my eyeballs. I tossed the mirror aside. It crashed on the concrete floor with an irritating sound.

In the dim red light the fiancé's round face appeared. It had a gray lining. His tongue flickered in and out, as if playing a new trick. I listened carefully and heard his voice.

"Why are you lying down? The situation in the family is very complicated. You must beware of pine moths. I'm surprised that when I was living in the temple with your father, I felt much more relaxed. Now I'm shaking with fright, in fear of stepping on a pine moth. They are crawling everywhere. Often when you're about to fall asleep, you'll find one hidden in your quilt. When the old fellow brought back that pine branch, I anticipated such an unsolvable problem today. It's been one week that your third sister has been eliminating those poisonous insects. Our quilt has been ruined completely by the beatings. She is never merciful, and she has a stony heart . . ." As he spoke, he lost his concentration.

"Do you think I have glaucoma?" Breathing with difficulty, I saw him melt into a shadow.

"Ahmm, in the temple, one heard the seeds of the Chinese parasol tree drop to the ground every night. Your father will never come back. He's got what he wanted, and now he's boasting about himself to the proprietress."

The very night when the fiancé warned me about the pine moths, I was attacked by them. They crawled into my quilt and nestled close to my legs, waist, arms—like a carpet full of needles. Turning on the light, I peeled them away and threw them out the window. Yet hardly had I lain down than they were with me again. They rustled; they pricked. I felt dizzy with pain. So I turned the light on again, and peeled them off, and threw them out, again and again. I was exhausted, but still couldn't sleep. In the morning, I found no pine moths but only skin made raw from scratching.

"It's tragic to be attacked by pine moths." My third sister

was staring at me. "There's no use to try hiding. You have to be whipped severely. When I'm in the mood, I often rip the whole quilt with my whip. Yesterday, I almost whipped the doctor's eyeballs out. He was in my way. Serves him right whoever dares to block me." Her T-shirt had dark wrinkles under the armpits. She was standing in the middle of the room with her hands on her hips. Her face had a murderous look. "In the temple, pine moths swarm out of the rotten floorboards every time the mountain wind blows. The day before yesterday I found that father's hair was filled with such insects. He was sleeping on the floor, and the moths were making nests in his hair. 'Jingle-jingle,' a little lamb was eating grass. When the wind stopped, the lamb would run very fast. Tiny pebbles rattled down . . . Ha, our father, it's extremely difficult to figure out his attitude toward life."

"I'd like to consult with others about our obstacles in verbal expression." My mind was working, yet my mouth was motionless. My lips had turned into a pair of iron clips.

"Hush." My third sister stopped me. Apparently she had heard the sentence in my mind. "Wild flights of fancy can only worsen your sickness. Let me tell you the cause of my asthma. It was caused by the medicine that the doctor prescribed. He was making fun of my emotions. What a fool I was to believe him. My heart breaks now that I think of it! Don't you take any medicine. It can only cause a neurosis. Never believe the doctor in this family. When you think about it, you won't be surprised to find that he is not a doctor at all. I believed it just because I wanted to. These days Mother chats with me about wild bees every night and about her lost wallet. I was moved to tears. In one stretch, I find myself walking on that stone path. When dawn comes, I realize that there is no wallet. She made up the whole story just to get my sympathy. Our mother squats in the corner making up such stories for others. She is immensely proud of herself whenever somebody is taken in."

One morning my legs swelled terribly, but my dizziness stopped unexpectedly. I listened intently. The house was dead quiet. Getting up, I circled through the house, supported by a stick, but not a soul was to be seen. I walked out the door and limped down the street. The sun was hot, glaring down from the branch of a tree. All the joining parts of the walls were puffing out dust. My T-shirt stuck to my back. Raising my head, I saw numerous blue and purple circles.

"Isn't that Ah-wen?" An old man stopped blankly. "Good, come and have a stroll. Good!" While talking, he scratched his armpit with force and then spat heavily at my feet. I walked away, and could still hear him chasing me and shouting, "Very good! Good sun, good . . ."

"Be on guard against such people." The old man's voice entered my ears like a gust of wind. "He sneaks into a python's cage whenever he feels like it."

Blood surged into my brain. In a hurry, I complained to a shadow beside the road: "I've been thinking of bestirring myself. I think so very hard. Every day, I hear the leaves rustle in the old camphor tree at the doorway. Just count how many blisters on my lips, and you will understand me. Only if . . . I've met so many people. I tug at their sleeves and mean to tell every one of them, but there is a great obstacle preventing me from expressing myself in words."

The shadow turned its back on me and remained silent. I could see the sun move to the top of the lamppost. The walls continued to puff dust.

"Good, good sun, good!" The old man was chasing after me. He ran a few steps and then bent down to roll up his extremely long trousers which were dragging on the ground.

The shadow turned back all of a sudden. His vague face was now turned toward me. He spoke each word separately through his teeth: "As a youth, you once had a food phobia."

On top of my third sister's bed lay a mountain of cotton fiber she had torn into shreds.

Somewhere outside, a black hand was scratching on the wall: *scrtch, scrtch . . .*

"It's a wire brush." The pale little face of my third sister peeped out from inside the cotton pile. "It's like this every night. It has aroused in me an unfounded melancholy."

"You?"

2. My Third Sister Tells
of the Load on Her Mind

This morning, after I scraped the mold from my tongue and cleaned my scalp, I started decking myself out. Under the lamp was the letter from my aunt that arrived yesterday. It read: "It's only because you've sunk too deep. You should rise with force and spirit in order to save yourself. For example, you can come to visit me and change your environment for a while . . ."

Bah, change environment! I am too clear about such rubbish! Everybody talks the same, because they all want to prove that they live in some kind of clean, high-class rooms so as to distinguish themselves. To such idiots, past events have vanished like smoke.

Next door lived a man who subsisted by scrounging through garbage heaps for odds and ends. This man had an extremely tiny face, with a huge mole on his chin. I never knew his name, since nobody ever called him by it. He was an independent, unimportant nobody. Yet I noticed that such people usually possessed the highest intelligence and the most definite opinions. When I was in junior high, he often called me to his house for a visit. "I often think," he said, as he stooped over to kick amidst the rags and rotten paper. The room was choked with dust. He was a hunchback, and the hump on his back jiggled up and down. "If only I could pile up all the odds and ends I have collected in my lifetime, it would make a gigantic mountain. I often lose my way. At those moments, I find myself hiding in a hole like a worm. Whenever I move my head, my face touches something sticky. Recently I discovered that the odor of rotten cloth pours out of my nostrils every morning. Maybe I'm dying. I've taken a new measure. That is, I've installed a ladder in the middle of the room, and I exercise while sleeping on it. From the ladder, I can see into the distance. I can see the fields, which are pitch dark, with some tiny lights swirling around. Once I fell from the ladder. That must have awakened your whole family, didn't it?"

"That's impossible," I shook my head firmly. "People in this house never sleep. Every one of them has some good game as a hobby. Please go on—black fields, tiny lights, and also little model houses? I've seen some little houses, in which people like you live."

"The wind is whimpering in the fields, somebody is smashing a rock by the roadside. Just wait, you'll see the rooster on top of the house. Beware of your surroundings. The guy above you is a suspicious character. I saw him with my own eyes spraying disinfectant on other people's clothes. Never dry your underwear outside your house."

The hunchback had enormous palms with deep black cracks in them. He rubbed his pointed ears vigorously with his hands until tears ran from his eyes. He called this "exposing the internal pain." He was forever wandering around picking in the garbage but never went very far. He was also a thief. Whenever he had a chance, he sneaked into other people's houses to steal an alarm clock, a tea kettle, and other trivial items. But he never had the luck to escape. When he was caught, he was tied high up on that big tree. Despite all that, people didn't seem to remember his past and continued to throw odds and ends to him. I saw him tied to that tree several times. Closing his purple eyelids, he would fall into sleep. When he was let down, he tapped the dust from his body as if nothing had happened. He hobbled into his hut and sat at the doorway for several days. He sank into his thoughts with his eyes wide open, and he smiled as if entranced.

"Why do you steal?"

"Oh?" He shrugged and paced the room. "At this particular moment, my mind is extremely clear. The little huts that you mentioned, I've seen them also. They were in the forest. All kinds of strange creatures lived there. There was one old creature with a pair of bear paws. All day long, he sat at his doorway studying ants and picking his teeth with a bamboo stick. Another guy caught passersby and tied them up with a rope in his dark house. Then he fed them a kind of medicine meant for toothache. There were many houses, resembling ghost's caves, with all sorts of heads poking out from the holes. They looked like featherless chicken heads. I was completely baffled by the scene and couldn't control my emotions. At those moments, I couldn't help taking others' things so as to stir up some disturbance and transfer my self-absorption. Please notice the hair on my temples. It's been rubbed down. Sometimes blood drips when I rub my scalp."

"Those ghost holes, they are so vivid in my mind."

The hunchback was gradually becoming senile. I saw him passing my house, clutching a wooden stick which he banged on the ground. He had become totally bald. His tiny head hung weakly on his shoulders, and his grieving eyes lingered on my doorway. I got so terrified that whenever I looked out the window and saw him coming, I leapt to the door and closed it. For days I would hide inside, and I vomited every time I heard the clatter of his stick. There was a rumor going around about the hunchback raping little girls. I felt very uneasy, sensing that there was some hint for me in the rumor. My body ran with sweat when I was in bed.

The second day of the rumor, mother yelled in the middle of the room, clapping her hands in joy. "I've had a premonition for a long time," she said. She also called in a doctor to check if I was a virgin, because this was "a vitally important point," according to her. The detective living upstairs arrived. He turned out to be the doctor that mother was calling for. It could be that he only disguised himself as a doctor. With a gauze mask and a pair of sunglasses on, he declared that he was living at No. 65 on Thirteenth Avenue. When he smiled, he bared a vicious green tooth on the left side of his mouth. I stopped him when his pale sweaty hand stretched toward my chest with a stethoscope. I told him in a confidential air that I had had affairs with sixty-nine males, and my state of sexual desire was extremely high. On hearing that, he beamed with joy. Narrowing his eyes, he asked, "Can't you find a small piece of wood to dig out my ear wax?"

It dawned on me that he belonged to the same type. The doctor told me that he was in fact not a detective but was only pretending to be one. Since he had to pretend to be something, he felt he was suited for posing as a detective. That was the only reason he did it. Yet when he was pretending, he did not feel at all happy. On the contrary, he was a little bit sad, because he was a man with deep emotions. Outsiders were mistaken to think he was indulging himself in the play. "Sometimes, I hate myself so much that I want to peel the skin off my cheek!" While saying this, he patted his chest bravely and continued, "Human beings should have their own personality!" His voice resounded in the air.

My situation worsened after the talk with the doctor. I always saw those little huts. At every doorway, there was a square table painted black. In a dish on the table was placed a heap of areca nuts. A huge black cat was snoring on each table. There seemed to be a pale woman bending over to tie her shoes. For a long time she tied, untied, then tied again. Finally she gave up. Her long silk stockings fell to her ankles. Waving her hand, she called me in. Then she whispered in my ear, "Close your eyes." She spat the dregs of the nuts in my face, one mouthful after another.

"The hunchback is putting up a last-ditch struggle." She listened attentively for a while, then waved her hand with confidence. "Just listen, the panting is horrifying. There are some people who are born being chased by terrible creatures. They can never escape. In their haste, they crash into the wall. I saw the hunchback pass by once after he hit the wall. The blood from his nose covered his face. In my whole life, I escaped just once. At the time, I was feeling relaxed. So I closed the door and made my bed for a rest. Suddenly a hand stretched in through the window. Whose hand was it? White and soft, it was the broken hand of a child! It waved at the window, making all kinds of gestures. Therefore, there was no use to run. My experience told me that instead of running, I could close my eyes and sink deep into a black pond. The days that I have passed so far have been very vague. I often feel depressed. Then I have the desire to look into a mirror. And talking about my mirror, there are some spots on it that can never be cleaned. Why?"

She opened a trunk and showed me a pair of worn boots. "Hey, my speech isn't clear, is it? That's because I have a little lump of areca underneath my tongue. I started doing that more than thirty years ago. At the time I had the ambition to break a world record. That was a good day. As soon as I woke up that morning I thought 'Today is a good day.' Chinese ilex was rustling outside and lovely red locusts were resting on my mosquito net. Opening the door, I found that thing was flying all over the sky, rustle, rustle, the red light flashing, and numerous people were rolling naked in the mud waving sticks. In the past thirty years or more, I have never seen those people again. That's why I keep the areca in my mouth. My will power is remarkable. Purposefully I sit in front of my house with areca in my mouth casting my frowns on passersby. Occasionally on autumn nights, I see butterflies all over the mountain. They emerge in an endless stream. It could be frightening if you were encircled by them tightly. You might be driven crazy by those little creatures. Nobody understands me when I talk to the passersby about those butterflies. I can't make my speech clearer, all because of the areca."

Suddenly a spasm shot through my left hand. I realized with surprise that I had been coming to this woman's house for the past several months to listen to her talk about her creative use of areca. And I had seen that pair of old boots at least fifty times. Every time I smelled the familiar foul odor. It dawned on me that I was having amnesia. It could be that I was not only suffering from amnesia, but also having a fantasy of creating a new record, just like that woman. That's the whole reason I searched around in shuffling slippers. I always went to the same house, yet failed to recognize that same moldy hostess. Instead, I mistook her for a stranger. Then I let her rattle on and on, only feeling regret afterward, and realizing that the hostess never changed. Yet the woman was not going to give up her talking. Her thick lips touched my neck and puffed out a sticky whitish air.

The days I spent with the detective (or doctor) ran in endless hot pursuit of each other. One day when I was washing my feet, my knee joint made a funny noise. With a bang, the detective fell down from the ceiling. Rolling on the ground, he snatched my shoes and ran away. The water in my basin was splashed everywhere. He had another ability—to hook himself onto flat objects, onto the ceiling or the underside of the bed, or onto the eaves. God knows how he managed to stick himself firmly onto those places. I guess he had suction discs on his body—at least three of them. His body had become lighter and lighter. He moved as if he were drifting in the air. I thought he might forget about walking and grow wings like a sparrow if this tendency continued to develop. My brother had been suffering from neuro-gastritis ever since he noticed the game between the detective and me. He belched crazily at every meal, burping up all the rice and vegetables he had taken in. Once, as soon as he started such belching, I jumped up from the table and kicked away the dishes. Then I declared loudly, "I have found a fiancé."

"How dare you take such liberties!" Mother shook her head, chewing loudly on a mouthful of beans. "When I found your father, he was no more than a chicken thief."

"What kind of fiancé is it?" My brother put on an air of surprise by raising one eyebrow. He asked, "Is that the guy who cured your sickness? *That* man? I've investigated him extensively. The two arms in his sleeves are only two wires. That is to say, he has no arms whatsoever."

"In fact," I cleared my throat and stated word by word, "it's that old garbage collector." Watching mother collapse, showing the whites of her eyes, I continued, "We're birds of a feather. We've been cherishing the same ideals and following the same path for a long time."

At that pronouncement, Mother choked on the beans in her mouth. Later on she was sent to the hospital to get the beans out. Hardly had she arrived home from the hospital than she punctured herself with her needles. Her body looked like a toad.

The first time the straw toy appeared at the window, I was having an attack of malaria. That creature was a man with a longish face. He looked funny with his mouth frothing and eyes glaring with rage. In the dark of night, rats were tearing at something. Turning on my light, I entered Mother's room. I saw her twisting madly in her bed, her pillows and blankets flying everywhere. As soon as she paused, the bed dripped with water. There was a small puddle underneath already. I imagined her having so much sweat in her body that she appeared to be melting. On the hill outside resounded a strange whistling sound. It came and went, whizzing in at one moment and quieting down at another.

"What wind is this?" The detective and I were squatting under a cotton rose tree, our teeth chattering.

"The sound of rats," I said with a suffocating voice, something pressing my chest.

The wind swept back and forth on the waste hill.

"Let's get married—it's neat and tidy." When he said this, his teeth chattered louder. I felt that all his organs were breaking.

Heavy, threatening footsteps could be heard. The shadow of the old woman reflected in the window.

"Of course you don't believe I'm a real being. You have a skeptical, indifferent attitude toward my existence," he said, still squatting motionlessly. "Not long ago, you told your brother while hiding behind the door that I was nothing but a product of the collective imagination. Everybody refused to expose the fact on purpose and pretended to be on guard, because they didn't want to appear ridiculous. I don't think you can deny that there's something between us. For example, we are squatting here together. That in itself indicates something. Your corridor is horrifying. One night when I opened the door, I could hear screaming and shouting from a battle pouring out like a flood. What magnificent things were happening in that dim light?"

That night, we whispered like two mosquitoes in the darkness under the cotton rose tree. The next morning, when I looked in the mirror, I could see scratches from the branches on my face.

"Mother, I want to get married."

"The cannas under the cotton rose were all trampled," she said in a flat tone, while digging in her ear with a hairpin. "Such zeal is frightening. At that time your father was not more than a chicken thief. That is to say, the matter is obvious."

I shouldn't have let that person stay at our house. For that reason, the old garbage collector hanged himself unaccountably. He hanged himself on our doorframe like a dried up locust. I had fallen into my own trap. After this happened, Father started to laugh every day, covering his mouth. There was a festival atmosphere in the family. Purposefully, Father and Brother would talk some nonsense in loud voices, such as "Hey, say, has that gourd you planted borne diamonds?" "Look, while I was asleep, three cats bit my ear during the night!" And so on. These conversations would end up in their nipping at each other merrily like dogs.

When he came, he crept in like a mantis, clutching a roll of rotten cotton wadding. Stroking his sparse beard, father sniffed cautiously at the cotton while clamping onto his arm.

"Hey, you, young chap, what's your attitude toward family and marriage?" Father pestered him, his leg sweeping out in a secret attempt to trip him flat unexpectedly.

At that particular moment, I wished he were a moth or something so he could crawl to the ceiling and scare the shit out of them, just as he usually scared me. But this weakling had already lost his ability at transformation. Instead, he could only keep quiet and crawl on the ground with his back bent low.

"Pah!" Mother spat at him. She kicked his cotton wadding so hard that it rolled into the corridor. He followed it rapidly and opened it up. Then he lay there on his stomach.

At first, he was completely quiet. But as soon as people dropped their guard, he started to sneak into the house, making a peculiar sound. It was such a faint yet sharp pulsation that people felt there was something sinister going on. Once a classmate of mine came for a visit. After she sat for a while, her face began to show surprise. She stood up and peeped out. Immediately, I knew what was happening. I coughed loudly, inquired how she managed to cure the tinea on her scalp, and asked her for a prescription. She tried to calm down. Stretching her neck, she struggled to neglect the annoyance. Then she appeared more restless, or even angry. She walked around the room, looking here and there, complaining that I was treating her rudely. Finally, she stamped her feet and called me a shameless liar. Waving her fist threateningly, she left the house. As soon as she was out, I went wild. I kicked down the cupboard and knocked over the tables and chairs, charging toward every possible hiding place. I dug for a long time, my cheeks red with fury, my bent nails carved deep into my flesh. Yet I could find nothing. The noise was everywhere, yet it was invisible. Touching my forehead, I found a smooth bald spot.

My classmate lived on the third floor. She, too, was a mysterious figure. Since she was thirteen, she had been eating a kind of tiny insect called sea ox. At the beginning, it was said that it was for curing the ailment in her eyes, then for curing hemorrhoids. In short, she had illnesses all over her body. Consequently, her pockets were full of the insects. They frequently crawled out and dropped to the ground. "Some people tried to take the treatment, yet they failed to stick it out. How can any treatment be effective without consistency? I have been persistent for six years," she told me upon her high-school graduation. At present I go to visit her about once a month. She is a small skinny person, always lying sick in a huge wardrobe. (Inside she has put a chair for sleeping that is made of cane.) The glass door of the wardrobe is always tightly closed. I can't figure out how she can breathe in there. When I come to visit, she asks me to sit in the middle of the room, while she herself remains in the wardrobe. We talk through the glass door. Even with her light weight, she has cracked the cane chair and broken the two back legs.

"Poignant memories!" She always ends her comments with this. Then she stares at her pale, transparent fingers, raising them and turning them around in the light. So far as I remember, she can only talk about one subject, that is, how lonely and damp it is to live in a wardrobe and how bad the air is. According to her, she is disheartened and has given herself up as hopeless because of the bad living conditions inside the wardrobe. If only there were any hope, she would strive forward and do something extraordinary. But there is no hope, not even a hint of hope.

Our break-up happened two months ago, when she discovered my relationship with the detective. I was combing my hair when she arrived. She gave me an angry stare and said between her teeth, "What a damp day it is today." She threw something wrapped in a newspaper at me. Before I could recognize what it was, dozens of lumps appeared on my neck.

"Don't fancy that you can follow your inclination unchecked," she declared in a shaking, angry voice. "Your dirty relationship has hurt others. Who has caused my present situation? Every night I bang the door of my wardrobe as loud as a cannon. I even swallow handfuls of salt. When you were squatting under the cotton rose tree, I shot at you with my air gun, you dirty pigs. Every day I risk breaking my heart. Oh, holy God, those withered cannas, those insatiably avaricious deeds. I've seen clearly from my window. Oh, Lord, please answer me if there is justice in this world! How can such despicable, shameless invasions of another's personality be allowed? My room is so clean. I hang two scented bags at my window. I change them every day. Once in a while, I leave two peacock feathers in place of the bags. The effect is marvelous. But now everything is gone. Everything is destroyed completely. By whom? Two villains without any ambition, mean sordid merchants! You will be punished!" She was heartbroken and left beating her chest and stamping her feet.

For more than a dozen days, I was unable to sleep. Instead, I hopped up and down on one leg till dawn, fighting with my life against an invisible little something. Eventually, my sprained feet swelled as big as buckets, and my body was completely mashed. I had to negotiate with the detective, intending to break our relationship.

"Help, help!" Before I could open my mouth, he dashed over to open the door. His yell attracted all our neighbors.

I closed the door and pushed it tight with my buttocks, asking why he was doing that.

"Fleas!" He stamped with fury.

"Fleas?"

"Fleas, fleas! You broken clock collector (I can't imagine why he called me such a nickname). Now I see that you've been hiding it all this time, pretending to be self-satisfied. Yesterday you were bitten while having a meal. You were so itchy, yet you only smiled lightly, saying it was nothing but a rash. I've been fooled by your family. How could I be so stupid? I get furious when I think about it. Oh, no, wait a minute. I'm not angry at all. I didn't mean anything when I said I was furious. Now I've become completely detached. I'm going to live a pure life, resembling the birds flying in the blue sky." Jumping up suddenly, he hung from the ceiling, swinging his legs back and forth. With a smile, he told me he was practicing some kind of breathing exercises, and he suggested that I try it, too.

"This is something meaningful. Ever since I discovered the exercise, I realize that my body glows and is as light as a swallow. The roles I played in the past are no comparison, just children's games. Your classmate is such an outstanding model. Once I saw her sitting motionlessly in the glass wardrobe. I was so touched that tears ran down my cheeks." When he swung in front of me, he kicked heavily at my shoulder. "It could be that you have some kind of jealousy about my success? Can I change my natural disposition through a period of hard practice?"

I advised him not to put on the disguise of a detective, because it was old-fashioned. He could have pretended to be, for instance, the night soil remover who lived on the fourth floor. That would have been more significant. After all, he was a human cleaner. He might have been spotted by others at the beginning. But that didn't matter, after a time of hard practice. . . .

"I've been pondering for two weeks. And now I've decided

to end our marital arrangement . . ." He swept through a beautiful dancing movement, stretching out his legs. ". . . so that both of us can start anew and live that meaningful, pure life. Just think, suddenly you can turn into a bird with spreading wings! Would you please not misunderstand me (he suddenly used "would" and "please" to me), and think that I will move out of your house. This is nonsense. I've made up my mind to stay on. I will build a bridge toward success through my diligence. I want to show you what a life with integrity is." He made two forward rolls in one motion.

A torrential rain came. Closing my eyes, I could see big raindrops bang on empty rusty iron barrels, creating a thundering sound. The white screen of rain blotted out both sky and land. There had been a similar downpour in April. The chickens blasted by the west wind fell to the ground one by one. A man with a black face and a straw hat was digging holes for planting trees. His hoe clanged against the granite. According to the old garbage collector, he could never drive those crows away on rainy days. They perched on the glistening sandy ground. They were so numerous that from a distance they looked like black spots on the ground. Their sad, shrill cries were soul stirring. My dream-walking spells got worse on rainy days. Day and night, I was constantly bothered by them. Whenever the attack came, I ran to the forest. In the woods, I smelled suffocating steam. The rainwater clinging to the leaves dropped onto my neck at one touch. There I always mistook the time outside as an April dusk. I always mistook the dusk's grayish blue, inside which there was a big pile of sawed lumber.

The wind swept from afar. In the darkness, the lion reinforced the wind.

The lion was speeding day and night across the open country.

Out of the sun's burned hair grew wild chrysanthemums.

The detective refused to come down from the ceiling. Whenever I closed my eyes, a pattering sound woke me up. That was him pissing. With the coming of the evening mist, he would start crawling back and forth on the wall, mashing the huge spiderwebs and threatening the fleeing spiders with a rattling sound. In the darkness, he would speak something unexpectedly. Immediately, the whole room resounded as if turning up a recorder. The hullabaloo would last till the next morning. I was so afraid of his speaking that I hid in my quilt pretending to be dead, hoping he would forget me.

"Your face resembles a green plum. It must be caused by lack of oxygen inside the quilt. To tell you the truth, I can hear your breath clearly." He exposed my mind. "How could I have been trapped by your mother and you? I have to understand that I used to be a carefree lad, shouldering my black leather travel bag, and putting on my leather boots. In my pocket, there were two quality fountain pens, and I had a pair of gold-framed sunglasses. I was such a genius in performance that everyone expected me to achieve some kind of earthshaking undertaking. However, one dusk, in the middle of my investigation, I entered by mistake a dim corridor, which was full of whispering, as if a mouth lay in ambush in the seam of every brick. You just couldn't distinguish. Now I am completely ruined."

Outside the door, an unkempt old woman broke a jar. Her shrill "Oh-oh" drew many gray shadows. I heard the splash of water and the sound of sawing and loud kissing from two old men with broad moustaches. The door was pushed ajar, and one of the old woman's strange eyes shaped like a hexagon appeared. The eye was surrounded by patches of dirt. "Aha, so this house is full of jars of pickled mustard tuber. They are stacked to the ceiling. No wonder the house is so bright. This dim lamp flashes so scarily . . ." Suddenly, she yelled, pointing at the detective on the ceiling: "What is that!?"

The detective twisted his body uneasily and mumbled, "Fussy . . . plus ignorant . . . What's happening outside?"

"My classmate is drilling holes in the cement floor upstairs," I replied.

"Oh, yeah?"

"She's been thinking of drilling all the way down through our ceiling. Then she would hang a wire down to fix you, so that you don't need to swing every day. Then you will be motionless like a thumbtack."

"So your classmate is a thief." The detective relaxed.

"Do you want to kill me?" My brother was suddenly heard outside. He kept one hand behind him and held a toy water gun in the other. He squirted the shadows on the wall while stepping back. "So you want to kill me?" he said again in a quavering voice. He made a heroic gesture, though his two skinny legs were trembling in his pants.

Ever since he was young, my brother had never had one minute of quiet. He was forever suffering from cramps, until he became hemiplegic. Sometimes he would sit motionless, appearing totally absorbed in thought. Whenever someone attempted to talk to him, he would jump up in anger and bite the speaker's neck. When he was in high school, he once overcame his timidness enough that he formed a glorious goal— to become a student of dream walking. "Then you can look without seeing, listen without hearing. You can wander among the black mountains and forests. It's such relaxation, and you feel so proud and elated!" His saliva splashed in my face enthusiastically.

For a whole year, every evening he sat in repose in one corner of the kitchen with his eyes closed. He argued that the atmosphere there helped him get into the right mood. One night, he played the fool by wandering along the pond. I gave him a box on the ears. He only stretched his mouth and continued his journey. He had to hold back the pain in fear I would see through his trick. I laughed my heart out. He also told me privately that inside mother's clothes, there was frozen meat. "Just poke your finger on it . . ." He gave a sneer of contempt. As for my fiancé, he simply pretended not to notice such a person from the very beginning. Always keeping his head high and dashing around, he never glanced at him. He once even commented on the matter to me by remarking, "It's said there's a person coming to our house. This is an outrageous lie. I've never seen him."

The detective became so furious that he blocked my brother's way. For one moment, his eyes appeared "surprised." That damned guy was putting on this show for me. He meant to humiliate me. He was wrong! I had noticed their jockeying for position for a long time. The detective was only an indulgent fool pretending to be clever. He could never win. The more shame he brought to himself, the happier I became. Sitting in a cane chair, I cast a sidelong glance at my brother. I encouraged him: Good lad, good job. Yet he was confused by this, owing to his rigid mind. I once saw sand dropping from his eyes, but he said that it was his brains. I cried in front of him in fear that he would die from this.

Yesterday, he was again in tears. Yet he also showed his teeth while speaking: "Once I close my eyes, there appear numerous bare feet flying overhead . . . Have you ever cried? I've been thinking of experimenting. Let's try together. For example, we can put a plastic bag over our heads, tie it up around the neck, and breathe hard. Or you can pinch my nose tight, and I can do the same to you. Let's compete for who will open the mouth first . . . I've been doing such experiments all along, and several times I've passed out. They said that a man comes here, that you brought him in, and he's staying in your room? Humph, I don't believe that you have such ability and interest. The thing I hate most are those soft shadows. They circle around you. They don't cry when you beat them and don't get hurt when you bump into them. But they scratch your nose once you close your eyes. Tonight, I plan to have a real dream walk. Don't think you can sabotage it." He kept his head high, his cheeks protruded, his mouth chewing. He looked like a wretched tramp living by begging and stealing.

I believe such rubbish was all caused by his thirst for sex. And such desire was totally imaginary. He had never looked for a girl. He just couldn't, because my generation in this family has no sexual ability. The cause for this was Mother's sexless reproduction. Mother was a witch, and she could even play such a trick. I can't help but admire her. This was why she helped so hard to get the detective and me together. She knew the result! Talking about sex, I recalled that old man dead of a stroke (poor man, his death was so unfair—why should he hang himself?) and the rumor. My mother might really have been surprised if I had had some affair with him. That would have been so far beyond her expectations.

The rain always came at dusk. Once the rain started, rustling sounds could be heard from every room in our building. Such minute sounds are mysterious. Taking an umbrella, you might stand on the street, observing the building. You would find every window covered with a black curtain. Some would be shaking because of the scandals inside the rooms. I listened attentively. As soon as I lay down, I found all the windows pressed onto me from all directions. I was totally encircled. The curtains rustled noisily until they broke and fell down. Looking carefully, I found under every curtain a huge mound of liver and a box of toothpicks. There was an addle-headed old man sitting there picking his teeth. Every pick was followed by a "pooh" toward the window.

There was only one exception among the windows. There sat a girl in a flowery skirt. She was cutting her toenails with a big pair of rusty scissors. At every snip she would clench her teeth and then a long piece of nail flew out the window. Raising her head, she turned out to be an old woman with white hair. She flung her snivel at me, then she folded her black feet covered with sagging skin. She yelled at me, "The conflict between us has no end, never!" To my surprise she was none other than my classmate. So I threw down my umbrella and ran back to my room. I can still hear her shouts: "Glass has started exploding!"

"So that's it." The detective fell down from the ceiling. He showed me his palms and said in a self-indulgent tone: "Please notice the two suction discs on them. Aren't they the result of long, hard practice? I heard you arguing with that female thief. I warned you long ago not to intrude on another's privacy. You are born with such dirty interests. Since fifteen years old, you have . . ."

"You have estimated correctly that the old man is very much to my taste. Gone are the days when I was happy and relaxed. I suspect that was a murder." Patting his belly and staring at the suction discs on his hands, I continued: "It's better for you to be up again. You've gained so much experience up there. I respect the strategies you use to deal with spiders. It's like the wind sweeping the lingering clouds. My brother believes that the thing on the ceiling is a shark with a monkey's face. Be cautious, he has a gun. Detective is not a role for your temperament. Nobody takes it seriously. Yesterday Mother told me that she remembered the master pedicurist who treated calluses. The guy had a pair of sunglasses. Where is he now? Look, she considered you as a chap treating calluses. What's the use for you to insist? Nobody believes you."

A flash of white light could be seen through the crack around the door. The air smelled of the wet rusty scissors.

A string of white teeth fell to the ground, and it walked smoothly for a distance. . . .

Pushing the door open, I stepped into the corridor. In the dim light, I saw pairs of bare feet lined up by the wall. The woman selling arecas was waving to me: "Attention, hey, just look at my cheeks. The areca is expanding inside. My tongue has no room to turn. For more than thirty years, I've been to the top of the mountain, where the ground is covered by fluffy dead garden burnet. When the wind blows, colorful little snakes slither out from it. I am creating a world record. I'll come back to finish the dream with you when I have time." She entered a room and banged the door behind her.

Mother's head stretched out from another door. She looked glum and said: "So you want to disturb more? You want more? Just smell, see if pine moths have filled your father's knapsack? I've been suspicious about this for a whole day and night. Yesterday he sneaked back once. I did not really care. He has grown so thin now, he did not really occupy any space, just like a mosquito net full of holes. When he left, he had only one shoe on. In fact why should he walk back and forth, what is he showing off? What? It is horrifying to think of the things that have happened in this corridor. No matter how far you can see, you just don't see anything, never see anything clearly, isn't that true?"

"There was a woman selling arecas," I told her. "I've met her twice."

"Hush, don't talk nonsense. That was your aunt." She winked and grinned. "You need to calm down. How can it be that you don't recognize her? It can't be more than ten years?

She is the same old self, never changes. She stole my lamb jacket when she left. She's been very greedy ever since her youth."

Mother's remark reminded me of my aunt, who used to live with us when she was thirty-five or thirty-six. She was a celestial, who could fly as lightly as a little bird. Her brows were plucked away completely, and her mouth was dyed bloody red. She nailed two big iron hooks in our bedroom, and on the hooks she hung a string, which held up a bed. This was her hammock. At midnight, she would swing in her bed as if it were a real swing. Standing on her bed and letting down her hair, she would utter strange sounds. Eventually she would slide through the window and fall onto the cinder road. As a result, her knees were forever swollen and bruised, and her hobby was hiding in her mosquito net squeezing the pus. To whoever tried to peep in, she would open her net as if nothing had happened and say: "Strolling in moonlight with neck stretching out, isn't that a spotty duck? There's also a shortcut that passes the withered rose. That path is a secret." She finally fled with a horse keeper for a circus. They walked away valiantly and spiritedly, smelling of horse urine.

As soon as they left, mother wailed and whined, calling the man "human-monger, with a hooked knife in his waist. Little sister has bit the hook." She jabbered on and on with tears in her eyes, but father was very excited. Standing in the middle of the room, he started his lecture. He talked about the beautiful wish, about the rats' invasion of the grain at our house. When he was talking about his painful itching syndrome, he became nervous. Rubbing his chest, he searched high and low, stepping on mother's feet.

Later on I heard Mother talking about the affair between father and the aunt. Mother understood them and supported their relationship in secret, though on the surface she pretended that she knew nothing. However, Father disturbed her plot. Nobody knows where he got this disabled man. The two talked in whispers in the cell for a whole afternoon before the business was done. Mother tried very hard to persuade them that I could substitute for the aunt. She said that although I was only in high school, and pretty young, I was very experienced in this. Otherwise, the garbage collector would not have hanged himself. But aunt was only a baby. She trusted people too easily, and she would suffer for that. Mother grabbed me by the chest and shook me, while shouting: "Just think what kind of person he is! Selling to a human-monger. That spider." For this she had profound hatred toward Father.

So many years have elapsed, and aunty has come back at night. With those mysterious arecas, she appears in the dim moonlight. I can never figure this out. I suspect that she never left. The walking out was only a trick, and the guy who kept horses for the circus was only a lie. All that time, she was hiding at the other end of the corridor, selling her goods to the wandering spirits. Though she was long past her youth, she could, with some fixing up, still appear a gentle and graceful lady. No one can tell about those things, because the corridor is forever hazy and tricky. Ever since I can remember, a damp steam has spread there. You couldn't see things three steps away, and you couldn't hear your own footsteps. Very often similar doors cracked open, and a soft shadow floated out. It gave off some muffled dream talk before it disappeared completely. Sometimes, I went outside. It was different from the corridor, though there were also those soft shadows. The wind smelled like a horse's mane, and the sky was pitch dark. Only those reddish yellow lights peeped out from narrow windows. They looked very irritating. When I stood on the low-lying land, I felt my body turn into a rock. The raindrops pattered on it. My eyes held water dripping from the eaves. A broken gong banged in the wilderness.

Oh, aunty, aunty, where are you? You even write to us, telling us something. You really take things to your heart! You attempt to fool me, making the illusion that this is a graceful April dusk. You think I will be running around like a blind person, twitching my nose to chase the smell of the dusty rain. It's your nature to put up a smoke screen in order to confuse human life.

Good, very good, aunty! I now understand the meaning in your letter. It's pouring with rain. A snake-shaped reflection flashes in the sky. In the earth, grass is breeding. The dream walkers are coming. Their stretched-out arms resemble iron forks. My brother is hiding in the middle. Yet he is no more than a sham. This is the result of your teaching. His steps are stiff and hard, lacking natural rhythm. I can see through him with one glance. Why did you teach him? It's in vain!

When the rain stops, I will feel my way to the other end of the corridor. I want to bump into you in the haze. Then I will ask for an areca, and tell you the miracles of these years. I will tell you how the detective slipped into our little house, how my parents disappeared mysteriously, how abnormal my brother's consciousness of sex is, how a cobra appeared in the wardrobe. . . . Aha, aunty, in fact I won't tell you anything. It's not necessary for me to fool you. Why should I fool an old witch like you? Yesterday, I found the compact you used for putting on makeup. I kicked it out the window. Now I still have enough strength to kick it. The wet rusty scissors have been inserted into the door crack again. The room is full of a fishy smell. Late last night, hundreds of nightingales sang on the tree. The moon was shining, the stars were shining. The little round mirror in my hand was also shining. Pale white sand stretched out into the distance.

3. The Detective's (or Doctor's) Long, Dull Story

She eventually attained her goal by shoving me out the window. The moment I hit ground, I heard her telling somebody in a nasal tone, "It's nothing, just an empty can. There are too many of them under the bed. They attract ants." Supporting myself against the wall, I stood up. Patting the dust from my clothes, I staggered away. I supposed that the run-down temple was just ahead of me. Somebody had told me that my father-in-law was enjoying living there. In the back of my mind, I had the idea of looking for him. I had to find somebody. How could I not? I had been deceived! *Someone had made a monkey out of me.* I had to complain to somebody. Good, just the person was approaching. It was a fat woman selling arecas. I had seen her from behind several times. I grabbed her and rushed into my story:

"Kind-hearted person, you have to listen to my story from the very beginning. This family is a wonder! There must be some guy hiding somewhere giving instructions. Once this guy blows a whistle, all my family's necks go stiff, and their eyeballs freeze. They are turned into nothing but empty puppets shaking in front of you. I've been searching high and low but can't find the puppet master, even though I've been severely tortured by him all along. The trouble is I have a little hobby, that is, chatting with others, and sometimes I enjoy playing a little trick. Otherwise life is too depressing. Yet once this guy whistles, the family turns arrogant. They march into the house and dash at each other, emitting the sound of cracking wood. It's savage. I have to hide myself every day in a cistern. Such long hours of hiding cause abscesses on my joints, and little worms crawl out of the abscesses. Unfortunately, even the cistern is not safe. The hermaphrodite of the family, that patient of neurosis, found my dwelling and drove me out with a broom. As I was naked, I had to protect my private parts with my hands and avoid his attack. He's a vicious man, so he knows how to wait for that fatal blow. He has particular hate for my sexual organs. His glance is too extremely horrifying. Oh, and there's something else."

"Aha, so you have recovered from your disease? Are you telling everybody that you have severe diabetes?" The fat woman pushed my hand away and staggered to the wall to observe me. She said calmly, "I remember you living by fishing for little shrimp in the past. You were bent down next to the brook. You slept under a dead Chinese scholar tree, all wrapped up in old cotton wadding. On that tree there were several odd-looking bird nests. The birds went into panic whenever the wind came . . . You once gave my nephew a bamboo hat. He's lost consciousness ever since he put on that hat. You've destroyed his life. I've been waiting to settle accounts with you."

"I'm thirty-six. They say I'm still a young man. The problem started the year I was five. Hey, have you ever heard of a disease called snake's-head craziness? It causes sores on the fingers. I had it once. It caused an infection in the lymph nodes all over my body." I blushed when I said that and kept my eyes on the ground timidly. I always feel embarrassed when I touch on the fundamental problem.

"You are learning a skill. That's good. I'm her aunt, and I've watched her grow up. The night you squatted with her under the cotton rose tree, I was spying on you in the corridor. I was thinking: What a good day you picked! I even pointed my flashlight at you, hoping I could dazzle your eyes and have some fun with you. You just can't accept the fact that my niece has lost her sexual ability, right? What I mean is that she has never had sexual ability. Why did I point my flashlight at you? Because she never keeps me, her aunt, in her mind. For more than a decade, she has been telling people that I've disappeared, and she even forces others to believe her stupid presumption. She has been sabotaging my little plans in secret all that time. Did you notice the window facing the corridor that humid night? I was behind that window the whole night, observing you two. I flashed the light repeatedly to scare you. I am the memory of this family. I'll die after everyone else." She glanced at me sexually, her wrinkles becoming moist. "Do you have any interest in arecas? All the residents in the building keep their senses with my arecas. In fact all those rooms are empty. I've felt my way into each one of them. There's not a single soul here. Sit close by me, I'd love to soothe the wound in your heart. I am a massager of the human soul." She squatted down against the wall. Her voice became as soft as a little chick's, and her eyes dimmed down. She beckoned me to squat down with her and clasp her hand, because she was having trouble breathing. She might have died if I had made any mistake.

I was delighted. This was everything that I could hope for. I immediately started my complaint. I love to start from the very beginning, which is closer to the fundamental problem, and thus more meaningful.

"I plan to start with the fundamental thing," I said solemnly, then I peeped stealthily at her. She was distracted, her facial expression extremely serious. I felt excitement rise in my heart.

"Thirteen friends have said the same thing to me: 'How can a young guy turn out like this? Think of the past, he was so valiant and bright!' They were stunned, they felt pained, then they presented me with a memorial album and an umbrella. Now I'm going to touch on the fundamental problem—my whole story, cause and effect, origin and development. But before that, I'd like to raise an important issue. Wait a minute, please answer a question for me: *Have you ever had snake's-head craziness?*"

The fat woman complained that some insect had crawled into her ear, so she felt curiously itchy. Shrugging her shoulders, she offered again to massage my soul. "I understand you." She sniffed my palm and put on an unfathomable smile. Pressing one ear against the dirty brick wall, she said, "There's all kinds of noise. When did you change your occupation? My niece told me that you've become a doctor? You're certainly very flexible."

"Oh, yes, this is exactly what I am going to say—why I believe that the profession of doctor is the most suitable for me, and why I don't feel that being a butcher fits me. The decision was an accident. It was caused by my mother. You know that my mother died when I was eight. Day and night, she dug in the garbage heap. She belonged to such a miserable class, and I despised her. At my house, there were always many female guests. They covered their eyes to play blindman's buff until each one of them was black and blue from tumbling and falling. Mother would boast while chewing odd-tasting beans: 'My child is studying law.' But in fact, I was thinking how to sabotage their game. I planned to pee in their plates, I planned to steal money from one of them. Outside the house, the sun was whistling, the little tree was swinging and swaying neurotically. I feared going out on sunny days, because I always stepped on my own shadow. My eyelids drooped constantly, and I always felt like peeing. I was doomed if someone gave me a slap on the back. 'What are you listening to?' Mother asked, putting her hairy arm on my shoulder. 'The shouting of the sun.' 'Aha, this child is studying law.' I walked into the corridor, hoping I would meet a person or even a cat—whenever I'm left alone, I long to meet something. I hate monotonous days. It's a piece of luck that I have this corridor. It's always so dim, and this is exactly what I like. Seeing a ball of stuff rolling by, I yelled, 'Excellent!' Mother and her female guests all peeped out to see what was the matter. But there was nothing happening, only my vision was blurred, and my throat felt itchy. 'He's doing research.' Pointing at me, Mother told the group, 'There's certainly much to do in it.' Spontaneously, they raised one finger: 'Hush.' Then they all returned to their hide-and-seek.

"I'm going to tell you in a minute how the idea of acting roles came to me—that was the product of a brainstorm. I once ploughed a piece of vegetable garden, do you believe me? Inside a broken trunk full of earth, I planted rows of Chinese cabbage very neatly. When the sun started shouting, I was engaged in an experiment on fertilizer production. I was very serious, yet very confused. While working, I was looking around. Every now and then, I would drop the rakes and spades, pretending not to be doing anything. I opened the window a crack and turned an ear to listen to the sun. When I felt tired, I would go to the house for a rest. But when I came out again, I found all my cabbages gone, only some traces of digging left in the earth. This happened several days running.

"Finally, I caught the saboteur. She was a woman who lived in a glass wardrobe. She was like a column of smoke. Day and night, she clutched an ice bag. According to her, this was her therapy. When she discovered that my therapy (planting Chinese cabbage) interfered with her therapy, she was determined to stop me. She complained that the smell I created in the corridor had caused a malfunction of her urinary system. 'It's no good to ignore the existence of others,' she warned me, while tapping on the glass. 'If you feel restless, you may talk to me. I will find some time to receive you. I'm not a rigid person bent solely on profit. Talking to others cheers me up and reminds me of my past.' She opened her mouth exposing her decayed teeth. Her face looked blue inside the wardrobe. 'What do you think of me? Not ugly at all, right?' Several times I intended to move, yet stopped short, because she ordered me to. From her wardrobe, she pointed at me and commanded: 'Halt!' My legs felt weak, and I stopped. My back was sweating. 'I have a classmate living downstairs. You've been evolving designs on her.' She gave a snort of contempt and then nodded her head.

"Thus I became a puppet controlled by that woman. She lived in the glass wardrobe, wrapped up in soft silk wadding. Her lips were black, her eyes closed. However, once she moved her stiff little finger, my body would feel paralyzed. Involuntarily, I went to listen to her teaching every day. Deep in my heart, I felt that it was something extremely important, and my feet simply carried me to her house, while my body was occupied with satisfaction. If I missed a single day, I would feel so agitated at night that I kicked my bed like crazy. At those moments, the woman who later married me was catching moths in darkness. If I stood up, I would bump into her knee. That was no fun: She had a gun in her pocket. 'Your classmate is certainly a circumspect and farsighted person,' I once tried to tell her. The consequence was a bang of the gun with a bullet going through the wall. In fact all I wanted was her consent, so as to satisfy my little desire. This has long since become a habit, yet the woman who married me would never understand this.

"The next day, I went there again. My heart felt apprehensive, and my head was empty, therefore, I had to go. This time she came out of the glass wardrobe to look me up and down attentively. She was in a black robe. She reeked of alcohol. Her neck was wrapped with a bandage, and one eye was covered with an orange patch. She supported her whole body by holding on to the arm of a chair with one skinny hand. She looked shabby and funny, yet her single eye was shining brightly. 'You have to change your strategy immediately and play the role of a doctor.' She gave me the instruction and put her other hand on my shoulder. That hand was dislocated, feeling like a fresh squid. 'This is a prestigious profession; I myself was once in it. You will be outstanding. There won't be any trouble.' After the comment, she suddenly turned very powerful. Pushing both me and the chair aside, she stretched her arms and jumped upward several times. She might have been thinking of flying. Then she stood firmly on one foot for a long time, totally forgetting my presence. When she finished this gesture, she reentered her wardrobe and lay down on the cane-chair padding, feeling for her ice bag with one hand. Her body was all wet. I knocked on the wardrobe door hesitantly. But she gave out a sudden yell and hurled a huge iron hammer at me. While I was running for my life, a big gust of wind slammed the door at my back, which caught my leg and broke my bone. It was very painful.

"One drizzly day, frogs were hopping about in the mud. As I woke up from a dream, I suddenly put on the disguise of a doctor. This matter was first reported by an old garbage collector. That old man was living by the restroom on the first floor. On the wall inside his room, he hung ragged female underpants, stockings, and bras. They were all covered with a thick layer of black dust. Every time I met him, I felt enraged. I often shouted at him: 'Get out of my way!' Instead of letting me pass, he would slow his pace. Using his wicker basket, he pushed me against the walls on the left and the right. He never talked to me, but only glanced at me showing the whites of his eyes. Or he would pass a stinking fart whose smell could make me dizzy for several days. When I saw his bowed legs and smelled his rotten rags in the dawn, my blood boiled. I had to eliminate this guy, who was a fish bone in my throat, an ulcer in my stomach. My struggle against him was a life-and-death one. On that significant morning, I left the house. When I cleared my throat to give him some warning, he cast a sidelong glance at me and suddenly discovered the change on my face which was going to kill him. I did not know what touched him, but he *discovered* it with a wink of his eye. So he started running toward the muddy field. Repeatedly, he fell down and got up, fell down and got up. Anyway, he lost all his normal behavior. I did not chase him but stamped my feet to threaten him until he disappeared completely. After a few days, he was found hanged on the doorframe. When I took him down, he was as light as if he were only a husk. All the junk in his house had disappeared. On the empty wall hung a solemn portrait of the great leader. Underneath it there were bloodstains from mosquitoes.

"As soon as I became a doctor, the woman's mother immediately proposed to marry her daughter to me. She pestered me endlessly. Once I was trimming my mustache when she dashed in. She grabbed the scissors from my hand and kicked me on my hipbone, calling me 'fond dreamer,' 'without escape,' and such things. I didn't want to marry her because I simply couldn't recognize her. Faintly, I noticed a pair of buttocks, a pair of skinny legs, and very dirty nails. Often I dodged her and hid aside, yet when I raised my head, I would still see one of her arms hanging on the wall, with thick black hair under the armpit. The inside of the fingers were twitching, and there were blisters between the fingers. I was greatly enraged by the scene. I practiced several times to drive out her spirit. Yet her mother, that witch who never shows herself (she told me that her mother disappeared ten years ago in the cellar), was controlling the unfolding of the whole situation. I could make no progress whatsoever. I would hide myself in the cistern for twenty-four hours, feeling relieved that they had started to forget about me. Just then the mother's voice started talking to me in a partly ingratiating, partly coquettish tone: 'My darling baby, I've been watching you. I've accompanied you all along. It's true that she is no good at sex. It's fair to say that she has lost all her sexual ability. That's why she is so self-contented. I am very sympathetic to your situation. I am a woman full of sympathy. Oh!' she suddenly screamed. 'You're shivering in the cold water. This breaks my heart. I've been watching you crying! Sometimes I feel happy when I see her condition today. I have to see her get married. If she can't marry, I won't have the face to live on in this world. Please think from my perspective. I originally intended to substitute her for my younger sister to marry that fellow in the circus, because my sister is a person with underdeveloped nerves. I've been taking care of her life all the time . . .'"

"Those people, she is addicted to robbing!" The fat woman suddenly became uneasy. "Let me take you to the temple." So saying, she started running, dragging me behind her by my collar. I tried to struggle free, protesting that I didn't want to go to the temple, because my life was hopeless. All I wanted was to complain to somebody. I was satisfied with that. "That can't be done," she said firmly, while running faster. When we arrived at the temple, we saw a woman with her face covered spinning thread at the door. She spat at the humming wooden spinning wheel.

I heard the father-in-law chuckling somewhere, but I couldn't see him. Oil lamps could be seen floating in the air inside the temple, busy footsteps could be heard moving back and forth. I had lost sight of the fat woman, but I could hear her giggling somewhere. The lights quivered. On the ceiling a huge black shadow trembled. It resembled an old bear. "What fun it is to fish in summer!" I recited loudly in a calm voice. Taking off one shoe, I banged it noisily. The fat woman told me that I didn't need to play any role. From now on, I could do whatever I wanted. Just like my wife's classmate—self-confident, firm, decisive. Before that, she had been controlling my fate. But now she felt tired and fruitless. Immediately, I thought of becoming a warlord. This was a role I'd been dreaming about ever since I was a little boy. I started laughing once I made the decision. Freedom tasted so good. "Your old partner is drinking lamp oil on the sly." She asked me to watch the big black shadow on the ceiling. The shadow was stretching and then shrinking. "I've been thinking of cultivating his son. I want to teach him metaphysical thinking, and other things, but I've failed. Now he has become a good-for-nothing. Look, that's him crawling in through the window. He cries bitterly every time he sees me and he chews up all my arecas. That's all about the family. You can't even determine what kind of people they are."

Finally my father-in-law appeared. He emerged from behind the Buddha. Shading his eyes from the light with his hand, he singed his hair on each of the oil lamps and calmly sniffed the odor. After some thought, he came to me. "You are forever thinking of floating toward that ball of light," he said, shaking my hand solemnly. His own hand was warm and dry. "I still remember you coming to my house to buy used pens. I must feel suffocated, right? It's very complicated. There's no particular benefit. When you finally float to the top, you feel worse, because you simply can't breathe. Some people died just like that. All in all, don't make trouble for yourself. But I, I love the little shrimp that are hiding in the cracks of the rocks. I am completely happy and pleased with myself. I swim here and there, never opening my eyes. That's why I never have eye disease. My legs are still good. You'll know it when you see me jumping. " He tried to jump up. I only heard a fit of cracking sounds and found him groaning on the ground. "I can jump really high!" He panted, waving his fists. I simply stepped over his body.

I knew there was something seriously wrong with his legs. What happiness and pleasure was he talking about? He was only pretending to be a young man. He could do nothing but burn his hair at the lamps and steal food from home. It was a life of penal servitude. In order to stretch his neck to let out the stinking hiccups in his throat, he used the words "happy" and "pleased." But he had overdone it, and now he could not get up again. Why was he so stubborn! He wanted to show people he was not afraid of death by burning his hair. But what's the use? I still remember his trick of declaring, "Going to the green mountains!" traveling bag on his back, that he had played for decades. Every time he looked full of vigor and vitality. But now even though he had given up the old past, he still struggled for a jump.

"He is living a happy life as a bachelor," the fat woman told me quietly, with a handkerchief over her mouth. "He is an out-and-out puppet, and he has lost feeling for his surroundings. As a matter of fact, his whole family has sneaked into this temple. When the north wind starts blowing, they hide in the attic. The lady on the ceiling is your mother-in-law, isn't she? Fortunately the old man doesn't know, or it would cost him his life. He is too solitary to measure himself objectively. Look at those oil lamps. They lit them. They light the lamps even during the day because they feel distracted. But the old man never recognizes it. This old fool always believes the temple is completely empty. I once gave him some hint, and he was enraged. It's so stupid that he believes he is unique. Of course, they can't see the old man either. They have tired themselves out with the game of catching rats. Now they are suffering from a bad cold. They've wrapped themselves up in thick clothing, and they poke their flashlight beams here and there every day. Bah, such people."

Night had fallen. I went out with the fat woman. The wind was strong. Creamy colored phantoms floated past us. We were huddled up, unable to see each other. . . .

I haven't told the story as I intended. I am forever circling around, never able to approach reality. Once I open my mouth, I discover I'm telling something that I have falsified, instead of *the thing*. The whole purpose of talking is to arouse others' attention. As a matter of fact, I never intend to tell anything, but only to make some noise. There was a time when I had the spirit to go forward. I dissected a toad, laying its organs on the table one after another. As for those little lumps, I broke them one by one with a small knife. We all make noise, which is very different from the noise made by rats. For instance, on a summer noon, we sit at home. It is very quiet around us, but the gal I married suddenly makes a thump. It turns out that the hook on her bra has slipped out. I know she does that on purpose, and that's extremely different from rats. When she has accomplished her success, she tells me that once she quiets down, she will smell the hair of her dead mother.

The oil lamps were crackling merrily like fireworks. The fat woman mumbled something and declared that she wanted to go to the lake. The lake was very deep, but she could walk into it. She had already mastered how to breathe underwater.

She loved the ghastly atmosphere. "My fatigue only attacks when I see black shadows swinging around me and bubbles ascend one after another." So saying, she hobbled into the dark night. After a while, she could be heard hawking her wares somewhere. The voice was disjointed, as if she were lisping. Suddenly I realized that I could never enter that temple. I made a circle around the wall but simply couldn't find the entrance. I walked around once more, touching every brick, but still in vain. Listening attentively, I could hear people talking and the oil lamps crackling. Refusing to give in, I walked around again, or maybe several times, nobody knows how many times. The wall was teasing my shivering finger with its firm coldness. At that moment, I remembered my ideal role. Also I knew that for the gang inside, whatever role I played had nothing to do with them. They only considered my change as a child's game. They always cast me in "the role of selling bowls of tea." It seemed I would have to circle that damp wall till dawn. Ever since youth, I had had a habit of splitting hairs, and I always stuck to some insignificant thing. . . .

Now I realized that I could only be a peddler collecting used fountain pens. Despite the fact that I made all kinds of voices—or changed roles every day, putting on a gunny sack or pretending to be crippled or swallowing down live snakes—they just wouldn't care. The key was that they couldn't really see me much. In the steam, they were busy washing their hair, breaking walnuts, trimming their toenails, digging rat holes, building attics. Everyone was covered with sweat. That day my staying in the cold water for such a long time drew the attention of the old woman. Yet she was not paying attention to me as a person, but to my pocket watch. She attempted to cheat me out of the watch so she could give it to her sister. She assured me that by all means the watch would be completely destroyed once it fell into the water. Regardless of my trembling from the cold, she forced me to give up the watch by clutching me by the throat. "What do you need that for? You don't even have a place to hang it, because you never have a body. But I can hang it around my neck," she said arbitrarily.

"He is nothing but a gust of gloomy wind." The woman I married made the conclusion peremptorily. "At midnight when I probed into his quilt with my hand, my fingers were frozen up. There was nothing on the bed. Something was swaying and drifting in the room, flocks of gray pigeons were looking for food on the ground."

I always change my mind on a sunny day. I consider such weather beneficial to me. Though I have trouble opening my eyelids, though I feel like urinating all the time, I always have some new ideas about something that I am interested in, and I always engage myself in doing something. When I am doing something, I feel myself as having a role. But I haven't been doing anything for a long time, because the sun hasn't been out for a long time. Now I no longer hear the sharp shouting of the bright sun, nor the south wind booming, only the giggling of the pigeons, as well as traps that are too numerous to be avoided. Now I am forgotten by them. I just can't give in. How can I give in like this? Tomorrow morning I will smash the tiles on the roof, I will let the panther in the corridor bite people. All this will make me feel that I am acting the role of a warrior.

4. MY MOTHER'S RAVINGS

I once entered the sun. That day when I woke from my nap, the room was filled with the fragrance of broad-bean blossoms. The scent had attracted a pair of butterflies, which were dipping and swooping high and low. As I touched my head, it gave out a loud sound as if it were an alarm; it also shone with a kind of mental white light. My son screamed at me, pushing me out of the house. "The sun is high outside, the rabbits are speeding across the muddy ground, the leaves are soaked with fresh tastes . . ." He seduced me. Holding my head, I stepped outside. The sunbeams poured down like running snakes. I remember I passed a slabstone path. The stones were so hot that the soles of my shoes were burnt. Every time I raised my eyes, I could see the pagoda among the firs. The pagoda was very tall, with a window on top. A man was experimenting with a tiny solar stove. The fire had caught his clothes. Behind the pagoda, the sky was all red. I began to run in a doddering manner. I remember there were some small woods ahead.

"It's not necessary to run. It could be an illusion. The forest is aswarm with rabbits. You might stumble over them." My son gave a snort of contempt. He was standing not far away, staring at me with two bloodred eyes.

I felt extremely hot; the pagoda was still burning, and the

flames singed my eyebrows. It was useless to flee, because the horizon was so far away, and in my field of vision, there were only boiling hot slabs. There really were some rabbits, yet they were all those unrealistic red rabbits that run without the sound of footsteps. Now I could see clearly that the sunbeams were skins of tiny red snakes. They wriggled across my hips every now and then. Each snake had a ball of dazzling fire on its head. They looked like stars falling all over the place. Yet my son was indifferent to the heat. People told me that every day he climbed up the pagoda to test his solar stove, but I knew that guy on top was not him. At home he always complained that my eyes were too complicated and colorful and "looked evil." What color would they reflect in the sunlight? I thought about this time and again.

In my pocket there was a small mirror. I looked at it and saw a big letter *E*, a black *E*. I turned it round and round, and the letter was still *E*. How could the mirror show an *E*? Yet I remember it so well. I tried it more than thirty times. In the sun, there was always that *E*. But inside the house was another matter. The room was cold. I put the mirror on the table, then I could see my dull, swollen face. Every time the sunlight passed my hip, I would miss something. It could have been a wallet, black in color, it could have been an old pin. In such circumstances, I would grab the person I met on the way and report to him. My talk was very fluent. That man would record every word I said with a pen and notebook. He was all seriousness. Frequently, he would shade the sun from his face with a hand and ask me that formal documentary question:

"What kinds of complications can viral flu cause?" His question stimulated my boldness further. When I got more excited and verbal, I would clutch at his chest ferociously for fear he would leave before I finished. The man did not escape; instead he became vaguer and vaguer, and his body became lighter. I knew something had gone wrong, yet I rattled on and on like a machine gun.

When I finally finished and raised my head, I felt my eyeballs were filled with different colors. My facial expression must have been like a devil's. I felt both annoyed and lost. Those people, why should they always carry a pen and notebook? This was something profound. They all had soft, smooth faces, and they could easily shade the sunlight with a thin, narrow palm. In emotional moments, they would instantly withdraw into seclusion, obviously to avoid trouble. At those moments, they smiled modestly and then disappeared. It is very subtle to avoid trouble: What kind of trouble were they trying to get rid of? How could they consciously realize such trouble was approaching? No matter how hard I tried to please them, they forever considered me as alien.

When I felt restless at home, overanxious from searching for lost objects, my daughter set obstacles to prevent me from approaching her. This disheartened me so much. Sometimes she would sit cross-legged and say in a lazy voice: "One of my friends covered himself with a bag that he made, like a silkworm cocoon. He stayed there till the last day. Even the fallen skin was well protected, and he didn't need to worry about the sun. There was nothing missing. It was just a joke."

My face blushed on hearing this. Consequently, I tried to avoid her. I was very careful. At the beginning, I sneaked out through the window, then I simply stayed out, wandering along the streets. The night was long and empty. I needed to find somebody I could talk to strategically about the Chinese parasol tree. The tree was very tall and straight. Against the purple sky, the leaves rattled in a loud voice as if they were emphasizing something. Every time I talked about a tree that could shout, my daughter would comment that it was a hornet's nest. She complained that I had something wrong with my eyes. The tree died the day she was born. What can I do to prove it?

Gathering my spirit, I decided to go and see the old house. I waited till midnight. When I waded across the drying-up stream, my legs were covered with leeches. The place was once a stone pit, but it had been abandoned. Piles of big stones stood there like dreams. That night there was no moon, and everything was quiet. I was frightened by my own footsteps. I heard a clang. It was a cigarette lighter. A short man with only one leg was smoking in the empty yard, but he disappeared before I could see his face. I gave a push, and a big pile of stones fell with a noise resembling a landslide.

Last night, I saw the camel again. At the time, it was very tall, shining like gold. I sat on it and rode along the wide avenue of the city. It was elegant and graceful. But as soon as we arrived home, it lay down and simply refused to get up again.

"Tell it that the ground is very dirty. It will stain its belly," my son said seriously. Hearing this, the camel stood up shakily. It stood motionless the whole night through outside our window. The whole time both my son and I were fidgety, discussing nervously what to feed it, how to manage its excrement, and so on. At dawn, the camel started moving. It chewed on the window frame then peeped inside the house. Suddenly it turned around and walked away without any hesitation. We lost it despite our pursuit.

"Where did you find it?" my son asked, grinning in a challenging way.

"It's been there all the time." I could not help appearing at a loss. I dug at the cracks on the wall with my fingers.

Plaster fell on my son's leather shoes. He stamped his feet with disgust and gave a prolonged "Ohhh" sound. He said, "In that case, it won't get lost. Take it easy, it's only gone for a walk. Did it feel very bored with you?"

In those days, I strolled along the streets every day harboring a secret hope. I gazed around, observing every guy with a northern accent.

My son tried to persuade me that the camel would never get lost, and I should stop wandering about. "How can a thing that has been there all the time get lost?" Besides, even if we found it, we couldn't solve the problem of its food.

But my third daughter never looked at us, taking it for granted that we were making up stories. She stroked her fingers through the air and said: "Camel? Humph! People will laugh their heads off! Just ask others. Where in the city can one find such things? I saw clearly that the thing you tied outside the window was a mangy dog. It ran away when I poured dirty water out. You are lauding the story to the skies: Camel! Stop fooling others, you will pay for the lie!"

But it really was a camel! Its skin shone like gold. It was so tall that I didn't know how I had climbed up. Anyway, I was on its back the moment I found it. My third daughter was too vulgar to believe in miracles. When I was on top of that creature, I even dangled one leg to show my fearlessness. I believed many people were watching. The bigger the audience, the more high-spirited I became. At dusk, little black birds with deep thoughts flew over my head. In the grayish blue evening light, the footsteps of the camel were as soft and light as if it were stepping on mushrooms.

I screamed just to draw the attention of others. My voice resounded in the air. A guy squatting on the ground smashing a jar remained indifferent to my scream. I fixed my eyes upon him, only to realize that the whole street was empty, and not even one soul was watching me. An old lady stretched out her head to empty a basin of dirty water. She didn't even see me. There must have been some kind of mistake. Residents in a city had never seen such an animal. They pretended not to notice it just because they were not used to it and they did not want to admit it. What would happen if they finally recognized the undeniable fact and if I made public the magnificence of my sitting on the back of a camel?

It had disappeared however. According to my daughter, I was no more than a bundle of rags with a kind of flamboyant character. Therefore, I decided to look for it. I had a bronze mirror, an heirloom from my grandma who told me that I could see a fire dragon at the very center of the mirror. I decided to go far away with the mirror. I still remembered that the camel had gotten up as soon as my son told it that the ground was dirty. It was such an obedient beast. But when I told this to my third daughter, she replied that I was finishing a dream. She told me that I had said the same thing repeatedly ten years ago. I was also making a strange sign with my hands (she tried to mimic the sign for me). She also told me that while I was talking, there appeared on the wall behind me a red torch, shining and dazzling. I was totally confused by what she said. Her specialty was to mess things up, thus making people desperate.

At midnight on the third, I heard a tricycle passing my door. At the moment, my sick ear was running pus. I pulled out the cotton ball, fearing that I had heard wrong. Pus dripped onto my left shoulder.

"Don't turn on the light, or the pigeon will be scared," my son warned me. I could see his apelike arms swinging through the air. He was playing at Chinese boxing, while mumbling about the crazy spiders that were running rampant.

There was a passenger on the tricycle. It was a short man with one leg. On his chin there was a big tumor. I could hear his coughing from afar. Once that tricycle passed underneath the grape trellis, leaving behind an extremely long shadow. It was simply too troublesome to move out of the house. It was not worthwhile to move those broken things which had no value at all. (In the mess, I threw away a kettle.) But nobody was willing to consider such a serious matter as the camel. When I was on the street, I almost broke my vocal cords from shouting. I saw only some very small images sliding by. They could have been some tricks of the sun, not even images. Pedestrians in the distance were as straight as poles.

My family members indulged in the foolish deed of feeding pigeons. At midnight disturbed pigeons would shrill as if they wanted to take the soul out of me. The whole house was littered with their excrement. Sometimes, they even sneaked into the wardrobe, attempting a terrorist attack. When I inquired about the pigeons during the day, everyone acted like a gentleman and denied their existence with a serious face. Pigeons? Where are the pigeons from? Then they smiled with contempt. By the foot of the guy my third daughter seduced, there lay a big gunnysack. Something was moving inside. I certainly knew what it was, but I attempted to stamp on it pretending not to know what animal was in there.

Before I could raise my foot, I was pushed to the ground by my son. They were birds of a feather. Approaching my ear, he shouted, as if I were deaf: "There are red rabbits in the wilderness. A mosquito is waving. Go there, it suits you."

To him, I was out of date, no more than "something old and broken" at home. My son understood me. When he was twelve, he got a big mirror and placed it in front of my bed, saying in a serious tone: "Mama, what a magnificent son is rising up inside you!" I felt joyful though I knew he was lying, because what he said was exactly what I was thinking. "This is not a lie. When she was young, there must have been a tremendous explosion in her mind, which left fatal scars. What reason do we have, as her offspring, to tease her? Who hasn't chased a leaf, a beam of sunshine? How can we stand the idea of exposing her last hope just for that and turning her into a beggar? Mother now is as weak as a baby. We have to treat her dearly." He was so full of righteous indignation that his eyes were filled with tears. Finally, he declared that he would "firmly share sorrow and worry with old mom" and "protect her fragmentary soul." Later on, my third daughter told me that it was my son who had "instigated" the fleeing of the camel. At dawn, he "threw stones" at the back of the beast. But I had many doubts about this, because she wore a challenging expression.

Every evening, the guy seduced by my third daughter swaggered in, his gunnysack on his back, waiting for the fall of darkness. Before the sky darkened, the couple was extremely busy. Putting on their big-mouthed masks, they ran in and out, back and forth several times. My third daughter was hot tempered, and she'd been afflicted with vain hopes ever since youth. However, this was the first instance of such publicizing. The most annoying thing was that my son might also have been in cahoots with them. I was determined to give them a blow. I hid in the wardrobe, waiting for that guy to release the pigeon. As soon as the little thing flew into the wardrobe, I grabbed it and broke its neck, then I threw the bloody body outside before going back to my bed. The two set up wild shrieks and howls the whole night.

The next morning, though their eyes looked like walnuts, they said to me indifferently: "Mother, such gloomy weather is not good for planting vegetables."

Holding back my pleasure, I replied: "Such weather is no good. I did not sleep deeply, so I feel very tired. I saw my camel hiding in a bathroom, eating the cement on the ground."

"I heard," the guy said in a rush, because my third daughter had given him a kick in secret. "In the gunnysack there's an animal that is harmful to the health. This is only a wild guess. In fact, nobody can tell if there is anything inside the bag. Therefore, illusions occur, gossip follows, unfair criticism comes . . ." He stopped short as my third daughter was ordering him to "scram." She complained that his mouth "stinks"; it was caused by "eating rotten stuff the whole year round."

In those days when I set out to look for the camel, my sister ran away with a geomancer. That guy had only half of a real body. At night, I saw him disconnect the other half, while talking to me offhandedly: "As a matter of fact, half is enough." When he lay down, he looked as if chopped in half with a knife. "Some kind of insect has grown on my body. They have eaten up the other half. The whole process was carried out without my knowing it."

Before the elopement, my sister and I squatted in the kitchen, discussing the series of strange things that had happened in the corridor. Blushing, she told me that she had seen a bloody rooster pecking the wood on the doorframe when she opened the door to the corridor early in the morning of the thirtieth. Headless nuns streamed past. "They looked full of thoughts. I could see that from their chests." While talking, she glanced at me in fear that I did not believe her. The incident happened one midnight. I opened the door to the corridor with a yawn, and immediately I realized that something had happened. Every door was tightly closed, yet the corridor was swept by beams of electric light, as if people were pointing their flashlights from above. This was very absurd. The north wind was blowing outside. A thin man came toward me.

"That's your son." My sister tugged the corner of my clothes with excitement. "I'm instructing him to cultivate another kind of lifestyle. Be careful, be careful, don't bump him. This is a successful try. Of course, I have to teach him how to wipe his rear end. I didn't see much hope at the beginning."

While she was talking, her body gave off the smell of horse urine. She was born a country woman. I didn't really see my son. There was a human figure, but it disappeared in a glance. But she simply refused to let go of it, arguing for my son doing some experiment. Then we stopped our quarrel and closed the door, because numerous wild pigeons had flown in. I believe that the pigeons were raised by the guy seduced by my daughter. This fellow was suffering from cancer, and he had to find a prank to cheer himself up. At the same time, he could create an atmosphere that made himself the center of attention.

"In the dusk, roses are blooming, wild pigeons are singing. You can't help feeling carefree and joyous," Sister rattled on. "Some people who don't possess a heroic personality have collapsed, and they've developed a mood of resistance. These people are determined to live a kind of nondescript, weird life that runs counter to both reality and law. The fiancé of your third girl belongs to this type. You can find such people every-where. They are easy to recognize. All you need to do is check their ears and eyes. These people are all cross-eyed, flap-eared, their lobes swollen and purple." Talking thus, she came over to check my ears. Grabbing my ear, she jabbed it with a hairpin.

"Bumpkin!" I yelled, and escaped from her grasp.

She continued, "There's a subtle relationship between protruding ears and crossed eyes. This has provided us reliable evidence. Talking about raising pigeons, this is an example of an attempt at self-exploration. In other words, the final result of the resisting mood. Such a result is usually interesting. I once had a friend who didn't raise pigeons, but instead just moved his furniture around and around. He was very sick. One of his eyes had lost its eyeball. Diastolic pressure of 110 is a separation. In the countryside, all such diseases will be cured in the natural scenery."

I should have gotten the hint from this (that is, fled), but the damned pigeons were swooping high and low, distracting my attention. While I was flailing at those birds, my sister blew a very strange whistle, forcing the birds to expel their shit. All at once, pigeon excrement fell like a storm. The whole room stank. Before I could climb out of the plastic shelter where I had taken cover, my sister had already escaped.

Now I remember the incident: The camel came here from the fire. At that moment, the sandy wind was so strong that I could not stand steadily. When the fire had burned to the top of the pagoda, a window below opened, and the camel stretched out its tamed head. The scene had stayed in my memory for so long that I did not feel any surprise when I was riding on its back. It simply came here naturally. Ever since its disappearance, I have been wandering around the blackened pagoda every day. I peep into every open window, only to hear wild pigeons flapping their wings in the empty pagoda, which they have turned into their nest. The fire was odd, as it did not burn anything down. When I asked my son about the cause of the fire, he was tying a slipknot in a rope and attaching one end to the bed. He asked me to put one leg into the knot, then he tied my leg up suddenly.

"Tonight, I'm going to tie up both of your legs so that you won't stamp on the little strolling parrots. All those wonders that you told me about happened before our birth. We were thrilled every time you opened your mouth. A few days ago, you broke the mirror, saying there was flame licking out of it. You are so rude. The mirror was our family heirloom. I saw you running around the house, writing obscenities with chalk on the wall of the public toilet. You looked jubilant when you returned. You even told me that you'd been to the forest when you lost your way while looking for the camel. But where was the camel to start with? I said so at the time just to please you. But you simply wouldn't let go of it, pursuing something unrealistic and out of date. You've become so crazy that everybody has a headache. Let me tell you, this so-called camel is only a symbol and sign of the color blue. If you are so foolish as to look for its existence, that's a road toward death."

He forgot me completely after his lecture and resumed playing with his marbles, despite the fact that one of his old mother's legs was tied to the bed.

5. MY FIRST DREAM

I dreamed an oval square with silver sand on the ground. Gazing into the distance, I saw the short black houses glaring covetously. There was no sun in the sky. The sand was shining as if it were alive. I put on my sunglasses in fear that my eyes would get irritated. I was not standing in the square. In the bluish white sky cinereous vultures floated, casting huge, dark shadows on the square. Then the silver sand would shiver as if suffering from convulsions. Tears froze on my cornea like wax.

"The wind is coming, Mother," I said somewhere outside the square, choking with sobs.

The square was very big. A stretch of black ditches framed the shining sand inside. The sandy wind smelled like granite. This smell was very familiar, as it often filled the air in my room at midnight. As soon as it came, three persimmons dropped from the persimmon tree: tap, tap, tap. At that instant, a black hole appeared in my memory, resembling the black hole on a lung in an X-ray negative. I had to open the window and take some fresh air. I wondered if many people would show up from the houses surrounding the square if the sun came out. Yet the sky was forever bluish white, with neither sun nor moon.

I mumbled blindly: "Now it's morning." As I spoke, I heard a rooster's crow mimic my voice. I knew it was my own imagination. The cinereous vultures were still circling mechanically. The birds had entered an extent of eternity. Their flying was neither fast nor slow, but always steady.

I felt scared after having this dream. Before dawn, an old man was sweeping the fallen leaves outside. These were big leaves from the Chinese parasol tree, and they made a big noise. A bright green star swam across the window, lighting the room for a minute. I heard my third sister curse "Damn it!" and saw her march to the window to pull down all the curtains in her room. She always closed the curtains after her dreams. Then she would lie in bed shivering with a pale face.

When I pushed open the door to my father's room, I found him not in bed, but in his armchair, deep in thought, his bare feet scratching the floor impatiently.

"Come in, there's a draft there." He saw me without turning his head. "Now you want to talk about your horror. It's like the black men in your childhood dreams. It makes your heart thump. You have no endurance. Please have a look at this pair of weather-beaten feet, and you will understand everything. We've all been there, your mother and I; those cinereous vultures are induced by us. At the beginning, we used to cry while clinging to each other."

"They often come at midnight." I sounded like a good-for-nothing when I started complaining.

"You should practice breathing in that odor. This is learnable. Your problem is that you lack exercise. Just keep calm, you will become experienced."

So that dream was not my unique creation; it was my family legacy. It was true that I understood everything by observing Father's feet.

"Are there residents in those houses?"

Father still did not turn his head, but replied: "You see those small houses. They are only the product of your imagination, because you are never on the square. We can only reach the edge of the square."

6. MY SECOND DREAM

It seemed to be midnight when I entered the forest with my aunt. The moon looked gray, and my aunt had big yellow flecks on her skin. In her hand, she held a worn rubber boot. She squatted down every now and then to pick up something and put it into the boot. I tried very hard to figure out what she was picking up, but failed.

"Aunty, what are you collecting?"

"Playing cards," she shook the boot and laughed. "The ground is littered with such little playthings. I am dazzled. When you pick them up, every piece seems to be an unexpected achievement. I play this game every night. I am so enchanted by it that I sing and dance like a little kid. But your mother never believes such business. I'm going to guide you."

The thick bushes opened beside us. This was probably a road. My feet only glided above the road, without touching down. I was not used to this. But the more forcefully I stepped down, the more obvious the feeling of floating became. My body was swinging, my long, narrow shadow looked like a guy walking on stilts.

The short figure of my aunt came and went among the trees. Her firm voice resounded in the air like the lingering sound of a big bell: "I'm going to guide you." She entered the thick black forest as if she were entering total emptiness, and she could still see the playing cards scattered on the ground. This was certainly a unique skill. My mother had a similar ability. Once I followed her closely and found her running into an empty deserted stone pit. She circled there several times and then ran all the way back home. As full sisters, their behavior was strikingly identical.

"There's a hot spring ahead. Do you see the spout of hot mist? One summer, lilies blossomed all around the hot spring. We collected them seriously, feeling really fulfilled. But when I got to the spring two nights ago, the old man failed to recognize me. Approaching him, I realized that he was chewing the roots of the grass. He told me that his two legs were rooted in the earth."

"Could the square be only a model?" I was still pondering this matter. The lily blossoms were another of my aunt's lies. The reason she left the house with my mother at midnight, sacks in hand, was to dig for gold.

"There won't be any solution to such things." My aunt suddenly hushed me. "In the valley over there, a rabbit once appeared. It was all red. Your mother went crazy because of that. One day I took her to the valley and told her, pointing at a protruding stone, that was the so-called rabbit. I shouted at her for a long time before I realized that her ears were deaf. Aha, a king of spades."

She was running far ahead of me, then her voice suddenly stopped. It was very dark, my head grew hot, and I pursued her with all my might. Suddenly I stepped on something soft.

It turned out to be my aunt, who had fallen asleep on the ground. She had her worn rubber boot under her head, and her fat body looked swollen and horrifying in the dim light. Without the courage to look at her, I turned around and tried to run. But I couldn't run at all. Anyway, I assume that I ran out of the forest and found a big stretch of flat land in front of me, and on the land was a tall building, with many open windows and irritating lights. Father was waving at me from one window, all smiles. On his face, he wore a huge artificial beard. He jumped onto the windowsill and sang out at the top of his voice, his thin legs trembling. I was hiding here and there, trying to avoid people and give my legs some rest. But lights were chasing me like hunters pursuing an animal. Then I said: "Now it's morning." Immediately I heard the mocking cry of a rooster. This method has become my magic weapon.

7. My Third Dream

I found myself living in a cave—this happened after one of my naps. I dared not open my eyes because I heard two tigers pacing back and forth outside. After a long time I was sure that they had not discovered me, so I opened my eyes and sat up. A beam of sunlight shone down through a crack in the cave. Someone was snoring deep inside the cave. He snored in his sleep as well as when awake. Touching my body, I found myself wearing a set of khaki fatigues. I knew it was only a disguise: No savages living in a cave wore khaki suits. The most they could have had was some hanging leaves. They might even have been naked. I dared not leave the cave, so I stayed there dully till dusk. The two tigers finally left. I could hear the noise they made while descending the mountain. I should have begged for something to eat at the foot of the mountain. As I had no preparation whatsoever for living in a cave, I didn't need to put on an air if it was only a fraud. I walked for a long time in the confusing mist, then I heard a weird chuckle: a human figure appeared vaguely in the top of the dragon spruce.

"So you are living in the cave?" he was shouting. "Excellent! It's very noble to do such a thing!"

I continued on my way. I felt very bored. I hated to see my shadow, because it too appeared suspiciously vague. This just wasn't right.

"You'd better get really prepared if you are determined to live in a cave. That will be an eternal silence." The man was still shouting; his voice was very irritating. I meant to hide from him in a bush, but he discovered my attempt immediately. So his shouting became all the louder: "Someone is in khaki, someone has a cap without a peak, and he walks loudly. Please pay attention to such matters."

I simply squatted down and pressed two stones against my throbbing temples. This proved to be very effective, for I fell into sleep immediately.

In a minute, I saw my aunt's fat gray face above my own. She was stroking my face with a pitiful expression. She spat on her palm and then applied it to my neck. The tone of her voice was very emotional and gentle: "You are beset with crises. Your living in a cave has aroused so much disturbance.

The cave is so dirty that I feel very worried. I plan to clean it and cover the wall inside with those artistic paper fans and also several porcelain plates. I learned such aesthetic interest from the classmate of your third sister. She is well cultivated."

Two pine trees had grown out of the run-down temple at the foot of the mountain. The branches had broken through the roof and stretched toward the sky.

Could my aunt be the snoring person? So she has been waiting in the darkness for this performance?

"Someone is raising two panthers in the corridor." She clenched her teeth. "That's the guy who was experimenting with growing vegetables. Today the corridor is full of disasters. The day the rain came, I fell asleep on the cement floor of the corridor. I shiver even to recall that. You have to be determined and persistent in order to live in a cave. I had focused so much expectation on it that I was overjoyed from the very beginning."

Many vicious black cats attempted to get close. I had this dream during my nap. When I was about to fall asleep, I saw Father's head pop in, hanging like a pine worm on the wall. Now, I wanted to go to the rock. I would have awakened if I had jumped down.

8. MY FOURTH DREAM

I once arranged to go with my father to the riverbank which was ten *li* from here to pick up shells and cobblestones. It seemed that we were discussing this matter in a bar. At the time, a skinny guy was squeezing onto the same bench where we sat. He was constantly picking his nostrils and wiping his hands on my father's back. Whenever we whispered, he would move closer to listen. When I stared at him, I saw that his eyeballs were made of plaster.

We didn't carry out our plan immediately after our discussion. As a result, Father made faces, passed code words, and made gestures in front of everybody, as if he had special privilege. I was utterly embarrassed. He even went to the trouble of following me everywhere. No matter whom I was talking with, he would join us. Holding my shoulder and winking at the person, he would interrogate this person rudely: "Hey, do you want to return to the joy of a carefree childhood?" Full of worry, I hid myself behind the toilet, hoping the big dog would appear, as if this would become a life-and-death turning point. But Father immediately joined me in my hiding place and rattled on about our "secret." While talking, he would elbow my waist, and ask: "Isn't it a wonderful break? Isn't it a genius of a creation? How did we come up with such a unique idea?"

The dog eventually showed up. I jumped on it ferociously but ended up in hitting my mouth against the ground. I made use of the momentum and closed my eyes. I knew that my teeth were bleeding, but I still pretended to be falling into sleep. It was not at all comfortable sleeping beside the toilet, with green-headed flies roiling beside me. But I couldn't wake up, because my father was waiting for me. Since it was a dream itself, I drifted into yet another dreamy image once I thought like that. In this dream, the earth was so covered with thorn bushes that nobody could move. Somewhere I heard a pair of bare feet running on the playground. The feet were full of corns. Because the feet had been stamping on the crushed stones, they had turned purple and brown. All my family members lay in ambush amidst the Cherokee rosebushes. The wind carried their whispering, and I could see Father's peaked cap swinging. (Ever since he got bald, he has been wearing that cap.) A pigeon flew out of a Cherokee rosebush into the sky. So there was another trick there.

A similar thing had happened several years before, when we were at the end of our rope, and the whole family fled to a stone pit. Hiding behind a work shed, we jabbered on and on until dawn. Outside the stone pit, there wandered packs of hungry wolves. The moon rose. I counted eight of them altogether. They swung in the sky as if they were stringed balloons. Somebody was taking aim at a black muzzle showing amidst the rosebushes. Father could be heard chuckling. Then a loud bang . . .

9. MY LAST DREAM

It seemed to be in our big house. The light was dim, and my whole family was dozing off on the floor. Half asleep, people saw a fine figure entering the house, but nobody wanted to move or to observe clearly. Nobody knew the time. The window was opened gently by the wind, and a strong scent of Seven-Li Fragrance filled the house. Gray and jade-colored locusts were hopping all over the place.

Father was the first to jump up. Looking around in a hurry, he put on his travel bag and ran out of the house. His long legs carried him really fast, like a master sportsman. The scent of the flower was making him crazy. His air of going ahead regardless of anything else was very surprising. Two big wasps flew after him at a distance.

My third sister got up early in the morning. She dashed over to close the window as soon as she saw that it was open. Standing by the window, she sank into meditation, watching Father's back, as if she were getting lost. She had once told me about a big snake shining with sapphire blue light. The snake crawled across the grass, its head raised high and swinging. The grass was very deep, with strings of ball-shaped fruit on the flowers. "Once there was a mountain monkey, which waited day and night on an empty hillside." Her eyes suddenly turn perplexed, making her face strange to me. The locusts were flying and jumping with a rustle. The wind carried Father's coarse voice. He was singing a funny song. My third sister suddenly straightened her face and walked heavily to the chest of drawers.

Mother was forever in a state of unconsciousness. In her dream, she stretched her limbs, and her face was all rosy and smiling.

I rolled on the floor and heard some disturbing noise. An old woman with grayish blue skin was squatting on the tea table, resembling a funny little animal. She was digging with her small finger in the tea leaves left over in the cup and eating them, while instructing my third sister about something. I couldn't figure out the strange language.

My third sister shrugged her shoulders, throwing the clothes in the drawers out the window. "It has always been placed in the last drawer, my model someone must have moved it. Damn him!"

Mother was perspiring. Her eyelids were damp. In her hand, she had a bunch of broad bean flowers that she had gathered in her dream. She was chewing enthusiastically.

I was killing locusts by the pond with my father. The sunlight was glancing on the quiet lotus. Someone threw a stone into the water. My father kneeled down to drink the green water from the pond. He said with tears in his eyes: "My intestines all have been dyed green." His thin hair was sticking out at the back of his head like the tail of a chicken.

Touching his travel bag, I found it completely empty. So I said to him on purpose: "It was said in the temple today that you were selling human organs. This could be a misunderstanding caused by the travel bag. Why should you take the trouble of holding it all the time? It's not beneficial to you . . ."

Turning around, he patted my back. He then sank into a reverie: "Dear boy, do you have such experience? There will be one day, let's suppose it's a dull day. You are skipping and running along the avenue, singing pop songs, even turning somersaults. Suddenly rain pours down. Pedestrians on the road start running, yet you stop in the rain. You simply pause, motionless. Thunder comes. You find a screen of rain all around you. Bending low, you pick up a spotted fallen leaf. On your feet, you are wearing a pair of rain shoes that you had in your childhood. One shoe is broken, exposing your bony toe.

There is a man, a beggar, marching from the fields. He is shouting out a song: 'The soldier's troop is facing the morning sun . . .' His rough voice scratches the milky sky sharply. Raindrops drip down from your coarse face. You suddenly realize that the person who is passing the field is no other than yourself."

"I've tried more than once the method of jumping from the cliff. But I've never reached the expected result."

He glanced at me seriously and said: "You have to make up your mind. Every expectation is a trap." So saying, he pulled away a big stone and pointed at a dead centipede giving out groans. Frogs were jumping in the lotus pond. "I'm not at all happy in the temple. There were days when someone kept banging the gate of the temple. I burn my beard because I don't know the time, also because of the feeling that the deadly silent mountains are pressing on toward us whenever I hear the wind. And the door is banged so loudly. Oh!"

The riverbank stretched out. Motionless willows stood on both sides of the bank. There was not a soul around.

Outside the straw hut, the blue-skinned old woman was squatting at the doorway, hammering stones.

The sun was circling in the sky. Many people were running madly on the street, every one trailing a long tail behind.

I approached the cliff again. As I was about to let out a sigh of relief, I heard my third sister's cruel mockery. I backed up in shame and turned around. Embracing her classmate, my third sister was staring at me with curiosity. That girl, wrapped up inside a thick blanket, was leaning toward my third sister like a spoiled child.

"Everybody is running," my third sister said, pointing at the streets below the cliff, "just like the maggots in the toilet. You come here, hoping that you can jump down lightheartedly, don't you? We've been following you for a long time. As a matter of fact, I've tried myself. But what's the use? It's out of fashion, all cliché. Yet you never realized it." She giggled again.

Then, sitting down on the grass, they jabbered about something. Their intimacy was simply disgusting. Mother was hobbling up the hill.

The Seven-Li Fragrance must be blossoming in some place far away. That's why the smell of our room always has an element of imaginative exaggeration. The whole family has escaped from the house. The deed reveals the fragile nature of our nerves. Every behavior of ours is frivolous. When I was ten my aunt told me, pointing at the empty corridor, that a fox had run into the clouds directly from the window. After the talk, I smelled fox for several months in the corridor. It seems true that whenever we smell some kind of fragrance of flowers, the windows open slowly, and insects such as locusts drop to the ground. Whether before dawn or in the boundless pitch dark, there is no exception. On the rectangular tea table, there squats a little ox made of pure gold. Whenever my mother talks about it, her eyes sparkle.

Everything seems true: The apple tree planted in the cement floor in the corridor is bearing harvestable fruit, a mysterious silhouette of a camel appears in front of the window, the blue-skinned old woman is flying with a pair of wings like a wasp, my third sister's fiancé has turned into the mask on the wall, and I am thirty-five years old.

"I gave birth to you while I was picking watermelon in the field," Mother grins like a mad person. "I can't count how many years have elapsed since these things happened. But you are clear about it."

Because my third sister saw through the business on the cliff, I have to stay where I am. In front of me is a desert stretching to the distant horizon. The brown sand undulates mechanically and softly, giving out a muffled rumble. I remain where I am. A turkey stretches out its blood-red crest. Venus is exploding in big golden flowers. On my left stands a parchment tree, from which there hangs a specimen of parrot.

ABOUT THE AUTHOR

Can Xue ("tsan shway"), a pen name that refers to the tenacious, dirty snow that refuses to melt, lives in Changsha, Hunan, in the People's Republic of China. Born in 1953, she worked as an iron worker in a factory for ten years and then became a self-employed tailor. In 1983, she began to write stories and novellas. Her first story was published in 1985, and since 1988 she has devoted all of her time to writing. Her previous books published in the United States are *Dialogues in Paradise* and *Old Floating Cloud.* She has also published extensively in France, Germany, Italy, Japan, and China. The stories in this collection were written between 1986 and 1994.